Sea of Pain

Heidi Stark

To those brave enough to face their biggest fears head on and come out the other side.

Contents

1. Chapter One — 1

2. Chapter Two — 4

3. Chapter Three — 11

4. Chapter Four — 13

5. Chapter Five — 18

6. Chapter Six — 25

7. Chapter Seven — 28

8. Chapter Eight — 45

9. Chapter Nine — 64

10. Chapter Ten — 66

11. Chapter Eleven — 67

12. Chapter Twelve — 70

13. Chapter Thirteen — 73

14. Chapter Fourteen — 76

15. Chapter Fifteen — 85

16. Chapter Sixteen — 87

17. Chapter Seventeen — 90

18. Chapter Eighteen — 93

19. Chapter Nineteen — 100

20. Chapter Twenty — 105

21. Chapter Twenty-One — 106

22. Chapter Twenty-Two — 108

23. Chapter Twenty-Three   114

24. Chapter Twenty-Four   116

25. Chapter Twenty-Five   117

26. Chapter Twenty-Six   118

27. Chapter Twenty-Seven   121

28. Chapter Twenty-Eight   122

29. Chapter Twenty-Nine   130

30. Chapter Thirty   131

31. Chapter Thirty-One   135

32. Chapter Thirty-Two   137

33. Chapter Thirty-Three   139

34. Chapter Thirty-Four   141

Also by Heidi Stark   142

About Heidi Stark   144

CHAPTER ONE

Angel

After napping for a few hours, I wake feeling exponentially lighter. I'm surprised I could fall asleep at all, a heady mix of adrenalin and fatigue warring over my consciousness. I guess the fatigue ultimately won out. Sharing my story with the guys was draining, each spoken word feeling like my brain was being scraped raw against a box grater as I relived my experience.

It frayed my nerves as I recounted my story, like wires spliced open with their fibers spilling everywhere, and I'm doubtful that they'll ever be able to find their way to their original places again. But, at the same time, it was also invigorating and empowering to finally get it all out. In sharing with the guys, I wanted to make sure every detail was accurate, too, and not gloss over anything.

They needed to hear it all if they're going to understand me, if they're going to truly know me. And there's also something about letting the words out that seems to have released some of the power they've been holding inside me for far too long.

I've done a little energy healing work before, and learned that when you cut a cord with something that doesn't serve you, that you should throw it back into the light... the opposite of burying it deep down inside, which I've been doing for more than half my life. For far too long. That by releasing the dark energy that holds you down even when the dark deeds themselves have long been done, the same energy that has been doing you harm can completely transform into something else. Someone can repurpose it into something positive, something beautiful. It made sense as a concept, but I'd never thought it applied to me.

Isn't it funny how you can hear about a concept and it makes complete sense... when it comes to everyone else, that is. And this isn't coming from a narcissistic place... quite the opposite, really. It's almost like *they* are deserving, *they* get to have the thing, *they* get the benefits of whatever that thing is, but you don't. I don't. This line of thinking is something I'm working on but haven't quite managed to overcome yet.

Today, I told the guys things that I'd told nobody before, and it felt good once they were out, even though each syllable was a struggle. They're no longer a secret, and no longer only mine to bear. I feel validated by the concern each man displayed based on what I shared. I'm almost giddy. Not that I want to go around telling everybody all of my traumatic experiences, but I took a risk and now I feel like part of a team instead of being so alone. It's a new feeling for me, but it's one that I'm not opposed to.

I've done therapy a few times over the years, but it never felt like this. I didn't feel nearly this comfortable opening up to a professional in a clinical environment, with their buzzwords and the way I could tell they were analyzing my every word, my every facial expression and my body language.

Sitting on a therapist's couch, it felt like I was being judged or dissected as a subject rather than a human being. It didn't matter who the therapist was, and I cycled through a few trying to find the right fit, but was ultimately unsuccessful. I was there for the hour, or forty-five minutes, or whatever it was, each of us furtively glancing at the clock as time counted down. Them, ready to collect their payment and send me away with some homework that always seemed too simple. Me, waiting to be dismissed, wondering what they'd actually have to say without their professional filter, their impenetrable clinical facade devoid of true human emotion. Some days, I assumed they were silently judging me, thinking I was some kind of lunatic that they couldn't wait to leave their office. Other days, our conversations seemed so normal, so benign, that I thought they might wonder why I was even there. Someone indulging in sharing their minor day-to-day frustrations for a while. So instead, I'd shut down and tell them as little as possible. It was just easier that way.

That's all to say my time in therapy didn't last long, and the many sessions I went to cumulatively couldn't hold a candle to the impact of my sharing my story with the guys today.

There was something else that set this sharing session apart as well. I could tell that any of my four men would have insisted on taking the pain I endured on my behalf if they could have, no questions asked. Their facial expressions and body language were so raw, so authentic. There's no doubt in my mind they're all in for helping me put a stop to my stalker.

And Roman's reaction struck me in particular. He was so compassionate and tender with me.

I feel safe with all of them now, strangely even Slade, which is a bit of a shock.

But I have unfinished business with Roman, and I could use a pleasant distraction.

Chapter Two

Roman

I'm sitting on my bed thinking things through. I press my back up against some pillows stacked against the headboard, and my legs are straight out in front of me. My body is comfortable, but pain torments my mind.

My room feels both large and small, and I think it's because my mind is actively trying to put things into perspective. Angel shared so many stories today that transcend both time and geography, all raw and real and horrific.

I don't get upset about a lot of things, and neither do the other guys, but today all four of us were. And one thing I know about us is that when we do get upset, it's for a reason, and this type of emotion tends to transform itself into rage and a thirst for vengeance. Nobody gets to make us feel like this without consequences. And this isn't at all on Angel, this is on *him*.

The horrors Angel has endured at her psycho stalker's hands are unthinkable, and each of us hung onto every word, every syllable, as she recounted the sick acts he perpetrated on her over an extended period. Knowing that he's here, on this island, continuing to pursue and torment her has us clear on one thing. We will end him. And it will be on *her* terms.

At this moment, though, I just want to make Angel feel better. To distract her. The only way that I can think of is with my cock, but that might not be quite what she needs right now. After all, she just shared some of her deepest, darkest secrets and fears, and some might think it's too soon to flick from those dark topics to something more primal.

Or maybe it's exactly what she needs.

It's abundantly clear that she's been wanting it, even though she's had three others available under this roof for various activities. Despite that, she's been clear that she's still craving me, but I couldn't give it to her until this point.

Not because I didn't want to. That's certainly not the case, and I've lost count of the number of times I've jerked off thinking about burying myself deep inside her. But she's different from all the other women because she actually means something to me, and it's been giving me some kind of anxiety that I'm just going to fuck it up.

It has to be special with her, because she's special. She's taken up an important space in my life.

Actually, that's an understatement.

Angel is not just special. She's not just important to me.

She's everything.

***

As I ponder whether to make a move, and as if she's reading my mind, Angel appears at my door, wrapped only in a towel.

She looks like a weight has been lifted off her shoulders from earlier. Her shoulders look visibly more relaxed, her upper body far less tense. She even has a cheeky little grin on her face, like she's up to mischief.

God, she's so fucking cute.

She's an impressive human, too.

Some people would have shriveled and wilted after what she's been through, but here she is, standing in my doorway with an energetic strength radiating from her. Dressed only in a fluffy pink towel.

That's it. It's done. I'm in love.

"Can I come in?" she asks, peering up at me through her eyelashes with the gorgeous little smile continuing to build on her face. As if she needs permission, and as if there's a chance in hell that I'd say no.

"Sure," I smile back at her.

She walks into the room and then stops when she's about halfway to the bed.

"Oops," she says, dropping the towel so that it cascades to the floor behind her, revealing her gorgeous body. Jesus. My cock is instantly rock hard. She's got my attention on so many levels. I could just sit here and look at her all day, although of course I want to do more.

Fast or slow, everything or nothing. I'm okay with whatever she wants as long as I get to be around her. If the other guys could hear my thought process right now, they'd wonder what happened to the 'real' Roman, or at least the Roman they thought they knew.

When it comes to women, the Roman they're used to has always been about getting what he wants, when he wants it, and it generally has taken little effort to get that. But clearly, Angel has happened to me. I'm still the real me, but I've evolved, and I'll never be the same. I know I'm not alone in this. She's had a significant effect on all of us. Even Slade, although he tries to hide it.

Her hips sway as she walks toward the bed, highlighting her ample, shapely thighs and the curve of her waist, her breasts bouncing gently with each step she takes. My cock jerks in response to her body simply walking toward me. She's just so fucking perfect.

"Are you sure you want to do this?" I ask as she approaches me.

She's the one initiating this interaction, but I want to be sure. Especially now, especially after all she shared with me and the others. It's been a massive day for her, and I want to make sure we take things at her pace, that she doesn't feel pressured to do anything she might regret later. She's had enough bad things happen to her to last many lifetimes, and the last thing I would ever want to do is add to that list.

Without responding verbally, she climbs onto the bed and straddles me between her gorgeous thighs, and I cup her breasts with both hands. I take this as a yes, that she wants to do this. Her nipples are rock hard, and I lean up and kiss each one gently. She lets out soft moans, almost inaudible, both times, but I hear them.

Although she's displaying confidence in her actions, I see a flicker in her eyes. It only lasts a fraction of a second, but I know what it is. She's worried that I might reject her because we haven't gone here yet. She's not entirely sure why I haven't crossed this line with her yet, and deep down inside, she's concerned that it's because I don't want her. That's the last thing I want her to think. I need to fix this, so she never worries about that again.

"I've wanted this ever since I saw you in the salon, Angel," I growl. "I need you to know that the reason I didn't try had nothing to do with you. It was all about what was going on in my mind, and what I thought was the right thing to do."

Her gaze locks onto mine. "If you wanted it, then why didn't you take it?" she asks as she undoes my pants. "And since when have you been concerned about the right thing to do?"

I slide my pants off, leaving me naked from the waist down.

"Too many clothes," she says as she glances down my body, pulling off my shirt as well so that we're both completely naked.

"Because you're way more special to me than anyone else, Angel." I pull her face to mine, gently kissing her. "I don't want to fuck everything up. You deserve the world, and for people to treat you with respect."

"So you withhold your cock? Unfair," she pouts, her plump lower lip jutting out. I can tell she's half joking. "I like that you respect me and all, but respect shouldn't mean I don't get to have this type of fun with you when we both want it."

"Okay, okay, you can have it now," I laugh, putting my hands up in mock defense and then returning them to her hips. "But only if you really want it."

"Oh, I *really* want it," she grins, reaching down behind her and sliding her hand along my shaft. I groan at her touch. "I want you on top of me, to show me you mean what you just said," she says.

Together, we flip over so that I'm now on top, my forearms propped on either side of her head. She's soaking wet, and as much as I enjoy an extended foreplay session, I can tell she wants to get down to business just as much as I do. I dip my head and we kiss. It's passionate from the outset, our tongues interlocking and exploring each other with a mutual hunger. She moans and wraps her arms around my neck. "I need you, Roman, now. Please."

I line myself up with her entrance, and in one thrust, I slide myself all the way inside her to the base of my cock. She gasps as I fill her up. "Fuck, Roman!" she cries out.

I groan as she clenches so tightly around me I can barely move.

"That's what you're doing. We're fucking and I'm Roman." I grin at her.

She rolls her eyes and grins back, her gaze full of desire. "I knew your cock was going to feel amazing."

"Well, that's funny, because I've been wanting to bury it inside your gorgeous pussy for days. I was confident you were going to feel amazing, especially based on what I'd heard."

"From what you'd heard?" She arches an eyebrow at me as if demanding an explanation.

"Well, I'd heard rumors. To be fair." I smirk. "No complaints from the other guys, only effusive compliments. A+. Five out of five."

"You discussed that with them? With Brick?" A flicker of concern crosses her face. I guess that must feel a bit weird, hearing that a houseful of guys are talking about you in that way. But it really wasn't like that. Everyone is just so mesmerized by her, she's become one of our principal topics. We can't get enough.

And most of it isn't about what she's like naked. It's about her interests and her hopes and fears, how funny and smart she is, how she's changed our worlds in such a short time just by being around us. By being herself. We're so lucky she's part of our chosen family. At least for now.

There's a giant 'what if' shadow hanging over our heads in terms of how long this will last for, and what will happen next, but as much as possible, we're all living in the moment, just enjoying having her here. We're committed to helping her take her psycho stalker down. After that, nobody really knows. We'll figure out the rest later. In the meantime, she's part of us and we can't get enough.

"Not in detail," I say, not wanting to get into all the things I've just been thinking about right now, but hopefully just enough to put her at ease. I caress the curve of her waist with both hands. "Nothing disrespectful. I just know enough to be aware they had a great time and no regrets."

She laughs, and it makes her clench around me tighter. Jesus, this woman. "Seems like a shame you waited then. We could have been doing this the whole time."

"Nah, it was worth building up the anticipation." I shrug, grabbing hold of her by her hips. "It's not like we didn't have other fun. And besides, it would be rude to keep you all to myself. You're quite popular around here, you know." I wink at her and she moans as I thrust slowly in and out of her, teasing her, not wanting to rush this.

"You don't mind the... sharing?" she asks, her voice coming out in a soft gasp as she looks down to watch as I plunge my cock deep inside her.

"If you're asking if I mind my brothers railing you, then the answer is no. I don't mind. There's enough of you to go around." I shrug. "Besides, jealousy isn't my thing. Any of our things, really. But if you don't mind, I'd prefer to stop talking about their dicks being inside you and focus on mine. Be in the moment and all that."

She wraps her legs around my waist and her arms around my neck, and part of me melts inside. This one gesture makes me feel strong and powerful, and part of me regrets not having done this sooner because we could have been doing it a lot this whole time. Then again, it feels like everything has led up to this moment for a reason.

"That's totally fine with me," she moans, arching her hips up toward me. "From now on, I'm one hundred percent focused on your cock."

I thrust my cock in and out of her, faster now, rolling my hips to give her a variety of sensations deep in her core. She moans at the change in pace, and a shiver runs through me as she rakes her nails down my back while I pump myself deep into her and extract myself again, over and over.

"Fuck, Angel," I rasp, my breath ragged from the effort. "I feel like your pussy was custom-made for my cock. You're so fucking tight and wet."

She digs her nails more firmly into my back and I feel them catch against my flesh, drawing blood, almost sending me over the edge.

I flip her over so that she straddles me, her hair cascading wildly around her shoulders as she smiles mischievously down at me. "Ride me, Angel. Show me how you can ride my cock."

She slowly raises herself up and I guide her by the hips to slam back down on me, her wetness and our heavy breathing the only sounds in the room, the scent of her arousal pleasantly thick in the air. I use my grip to impale her repeatedly on my shaft, and she gasps each time I bury myself inside her from below.

She angles her hips ever so slightly so I can get a little deeper.

"Good girl," I growl. "Angle yourself so that your clit rubs against me, just the way I know you like it. Use me."

I'm guessing, but I seem to be on the right track as she grinds herself on me, and I loosen my grip on her hips, letting her take control and work herself into a frenzy. She moans and I know that she's close, her speed increasing and the pressure of her grinding continuing to build.

"Fuck, you feel amazing, Angel," I groan. "I'm so close."

"So do you, Roman," she cries out. "And so am I."

She tilts her head back and cries out again as her pussy seizes around me, and I feel her spasm wildly, shuddering as she comes, releasing her juices all over my cock. Her eyes roll back and her mouth opens as she reaches her peak and she continues to clench around me.

As her orgasm subsides, I grab her once again firmly by the hips. She gasps as I hold her still while I fuck her from below, driving my cock into her over and over again until I release deep inside her.

I kiss her gently on her gorgeous lips once more, and then gently pull her off me and bring her to lie in the nook of my arm as we both regain control of our breathing. She nestles in, fitting perfectly into the curve of my armpit, and smiles up at me. Another little piece of my heart feels like it's melting. She's global warming and I'm an iceberg. I'm completely screwed, but I'm okay with that.

"You felt even better than I thought you would, baby," I say, smiling back at her.

"Oh, you're saying you like my pussy?" She curves it in toward me so that it gently touches against my hip, as if to make sure I know exactly what she's talking about.

I bite my lower lip. "I fucking love your pussy, Angel." Reaching up with both hands, I play with her nipples. "I'm going to spend the rest of my life thinking about how much I want to be buried deep inside you twenty-four seven."

"That's high praise from someone with your... experience," she grins up at me, her eyes sparkling through her gorgeous dark lashes.

I pick up a pillow and smack her gently with it. She laughs, hopping off me and laying down beside me, and snuggles into the nook of my arm. It feels so good, just laying here like this, basking in the afterglow of fantastic sex with this beautiful creature.

I pull her closer and close my eyes.

I don't tell her it's not just her pussy that I love.

I'm pretty infatuated, some might even say obsessed, with everything else about her, too.

Chapter Three

Aidan

"Where are they?" I glance into the living room and the kitchen, but both rooms are empty. I haven't seen or heard from Angel or Roman for a while, and it's making me nervous. She's at huge risk right now, with her psycho stalker on the loose and all, and the last thing we need is for Roman to take her somewhere that makes her vulnerable to an attack. I also like to know where the guys are, and if Roman has gone on some job without at least mentioning it, let alone a vigilante mission, I'm going to be pissed.

"I have no idea. It's weirdly quiet in here," Brick shrugs and randomly opens the pantry as if they might be hiding in there. He picks up a container of Lucky Charms and shakes it.

"What are you doing, Brick? You think they're hiding in there with the marshmallows?" I arch an eyebrow.

"You never know," he says, shrugging and continuing to shake the container and peer inside. "Worth a check. Weirder things have been known to happen around here. Imagine if they found a way to make themselves tiny, though, the size of the cereal. Like with a miniaturization machine or something. It would make for a good hiding place, a box of Lucky Charms. Unless somebody didn't know and they poured you into a cereal bowl, poured milk over you and ate you, I guess. That wouldn't be a good ending."

I smirk and shake my head. This guy. I have no idea where he comes up with this shit.

"Do you think they went out somewhere?" Slade asks, glancing toward the front door. "Roman had said something about needing to do inventory at the club sometime soon. And I know Angel likes to get out of the house more than she's been able to lately."

"I fucking hope not," I huff. "It looked like all the cars were here, and I'd like to think they're not that stupid. Besides, I strictly told them to stay put. That lunatic seems to be getting closer. We need to be on the lookout for any potential traps. They'd be putting us all at risk if they decided to get up and go just because they felt like it, especially without telling us."

I walk up the stairs to the hallway, and Brick and Slade follow along behind. It's silent up here as well, except for the sounds of our footsteps and the rustle of our clothing as we walk.

As I pass Roman's door, I notice it's slightly ajar and there are faint sounds coming from inside. I peek in.

He and Angel are both in there laying on Roman's bed. I turn and gesture to the guys to be quiet, but show I've found them by pointing into the room so they can also see.

They peek in and see Angel, fast asleep with Roman's arm wrapped around underneath her, snuggling into him, her leg wrapped comfortably over his, both breathing softly. Slade and Brick turn around and raise their eyebrows at me, and I nod.

"Jesus, he's got it bad," says Slade in a low, deep voice.

"I know, her knee is like snuggled up into his balls," says Brick, staring at their human origami. "And that's his cardinal rule. Always send them home after fucking. Never let them sleep over in case they catch feelings."

"I think you were right to be worried, Slade," I sigh, observing how peaceful they look snuggled in each other's arms. "Because Roman, playboy extraordinaire, appears to have been the one who's broken his own rule and caught feelings."

What I don't say out loud, and what I try to keep to myself as I wrestle with it internally, is that so have I.

Maybe we all have at this point.

In other words, maybe we're all completely fucked.

CHAPTER FOUR

Slade

The next day

I walk into the main dining room where the other guys are sitting, preparing for the day ahead. We have actual business to do today, more than just being distracted by a girl.

They look up and see my facial expression, their backs all straightening. They can tell something is up.

"What's going on, man?" Aidan asks, his brow furrowed.

I clear my throat.

"Zero's men have intercepted one of our hauls from the mainland. Somehow they found out where the drop was taking place, yet again." I sigh as I say it, not enjoying being the bearer of bad news. "We have to make them pay. And then, at some point, we need to figure out how they're getting this intel."

"Jesus, didn't we just shut down another major supplier?" Brick growls. "Do they just keep creeping out of the woodwork and taking each other's places? It seems like a never-ending cycle."

"Yeah, that's how this works, man." He knows how this works, but I can understand his questioning it. It's like whack-a-mole all up in here with these mafia guys. New versions just keep coming and coming and coming, no matter how many you knock down. They're relatively indiscernible from each other, but some just wear better suits.

"It's fucking annoying, if you ask me." Brick has a tendency to pout, a bit kid-like, and today is no exception. "I mean, send them all my way and I'll have some fun, but I like to feel like we're making some kind of progress."

I tap him on the shoulder for reassurance. "You can say that again, bud. We are making progress, though. Today, for instance, and what we're about to do. Let's go."

We don vests and grab our weapons and head out into the car. Guns are the appropriate choice for this mission, and fortunately, we have plenty. Normally Aidan would already be inside, waiting for us in the driver's seat, but he's not today, so I hop in and take the wheel.

After a brief drive to an adjacent neighborhood, we reach Zero's location. It's not a secret where he lives. It's a big place, and he's proud of what he does and who he is to the island. He's just powerful enough to be annoying and just a little dangerous.

Their compound is lit up with perimeter lights. It's a large residential building, originally historic architecture but with a variety of contemporary-looking wings have been added over time. Tall hedges that partially obscure even taller fences line the property, and the fences are topped with razor wire. Several security cameras are perched high on poles. I know they have a giant security detail keeping tabs on the property 24/7.

Of course, they see us coming. Zero's guards pour out of the building as soon as we pull up, all heavily armed as expected.

Brick and I pick them off one by one. Normally, we'd have Aidan here to call out positions, but he was busy, and we actually feel comfortable going in just the two of us this time. Generally, we're like a well-oiled machine, Aidan's leadership and knack for understanding how humans move, and Brick's and my precision shooting. It feels a bit like a video game, but with more grunting noises and a little less blood. Today, it's just Brick and me and our instincts. The fact Aidan didn't insist on coming to chaperone us was actually a compliment to us, a testament of his confidence in our skills.

When the guards out front are on the ground and have all mostly stopped moving, Brick keys in a code and the gate opens. He might be crazy, but he can get into just about any building regardless of the security system, and that's an extremely useful skill to have in so many situations. Even if it means you end up subjected to the odd lecture on veganism and animal rights.

A couple of guys are groaning on the ground and we put them out of their misery. For a moment, things are silent except for our breathing and our footsteps.

We step over the bodies and enter the house.

We sweep the bottom floor and it's clear, and the two of us slowly climb the stairs.

At the top of the stairs, we find ourselves in a long hallway with three doors on either side. The house is silent, but we know Zero is in here, no doubt with some of his toughest goons. These guys are highly predictable, leaving their weakest out front and having their most powerful men glued to their hip at all times.

We kick open the first door on the left, and it's a fairly empty room. It looks like a guest bedroom largely devoid of personality, furnished only with a bed and some side tables. It's immaculately made up and as if nobody has ever stayed in it. Some cookie-cutter-looking artwork hangs on the walls, and some generic books sit on the nightstand. We check under the bed and in the closet, but both are clear.

We kick open the second door. It's another bedroom, but it looks like someone has been sleeping in it recently judging by the tangled sheets strewn across the bed and clothing crumpled on the floor. We hear rustling from somewhere inside the space. Brick yanks the closet door open to reveal a man hiding in it. He whimpers when he sees Brick and the unhinged grin stretched across his face.

Without wasting a moment, Brick shoots at him, exploding the guy's head, and his body instantly crumples to the floor. Brick turns around to face me and he's splattered with blood. He grins at me, and his teeth are red. He looks like an absolute lunatic. Like himself, in other words. In his happy place.

The third door squeaks open and disappointingly, it's only a linen closet, items neatly folded in tidy rows, the potent scent of laundry detergent permeating the small space. I move a couple of items around just to make sure there's nothing hidden behind them, but it's just full of sheets and towels and regular household items.

Behind the fourth door is a bathroom. The room is clean and impersonal, only a couple of toothbrushes in a holder and a towel on a rack that looks like it's been hastily folded, showing it's ever been used. The room is obviously empty. This is disappointing. I want to hurt someone.

We creep along the dimly hit hallway to the fifth door. If there's someone behind it, they've got to know this is the next door we'll be opening. We've been coming down the hallway in sequence, left to right. Whoever is in there will almost definitely be armed, so we need to be careful.

I nod at Brick. He reaches out a hand and flicks the door handle, sending the door open, and leaps back. Gunshots ring out, bullets spraying the wall opposite the door. We're on either side of the door as a line of goons comes running out, at least six of them, and we pick them off one by one, taking care not to accidentally shoot right through one of them and hurt each other. Their defenses are terrible, and they're like lemmings running out in a row, easy pickings. Once they're all on the floor, we step over their bodies and collect a couple of their guns as backup.

That leaves one more door. Door number six. Zero has to be in here.

Brick carefully leans in and flicks this door open as well, but this time there's no hail of gunfire. I carefully peer inside, and Zero is calmly sitting in an executive chair, flanked by three more goons. These guys look more sinister than the last group, and they're heavily armed. Unlike the others, they're in full defense mode, and there's no chance of them making the first move. They're here to protect their leader, but on his terms. It feels like maybe he has something to say before this goes down, or they would have started shooting already.

Zero is behind a large, ornate desk that dominates the space, and he leans forward and crosses his arms on top of it. He's a muscular man of medium height, wearing a dark blue suit. His attire is obviously custom made, clinging to his well-developed torso and biceps just the right amount. I can picture an older lady stretching a measuring tape across him to make sure everything is exactly to measure, making sure everything is just right. Okay, that's weird, Slade. Get a grip. You're here to kill this guy, not visualize him with random seamstresses.

"I thought you'd never arrive," he says, calmly, even though we just tore up his house and killed nearly all of his men. "Men?"

I guess that's his cue. There's suddenly a massive flash and an explosion, and both Brick and I jump back as smoke fills the hallway. Coughing, I shield my eyes and then a bullet flies right past me. Fuck! It must have been a flash-bang grenade, and the goons are shooting at us. Clearly, they're copying Brick's chaotic style. I dodge and weave as I try to get my bearings. We need to be careful or Brick and I might end up shooting each other because of all the smoke.

"Ca-caw!" Brick shrieks, and I fly to the ground. I know his code. Two silenced shots take down two of the goons. As I get to my feet, the smoke clears and I see the third goon standing behind him, aiming his gun at Brick.

"Duck!" Brick immediately dives to the ground and I shoot. The third goon groans and lets out a gurgling sound as the bullet nicks his neck, blood spurting from the wound. He crumples to the floor.

This just leaves Zero.

He's still sitting at his desk, but he's looking very pale and fidgeting with his hands. I think he was expecting his guys to take us down pretty easily, judging by how he's looking right now. His confidence is gone, and he no longer seems so poised. I'm still not sure why he had his goons pause before opening fire. He said nothing profound before the flash-bang grenade went off.

"You know why we're here, Zero?" I growl.

He gestures around. "You enjoy interior decorating?" It's a feeble attempt at a joke, and I can see the fear radiating from his eyes. "You like what I've done with the place?" His voice squeaks, betraying him and his attempt to show confidence.

"Stop with the attempt at small talk or humor or whatever the fuck that is," I growl, my voice low. "You stole from us, Zero. We really don't like it when people steal from us."

"I—I—." His eyes fall to the ground and then flicker up to meet mine, but he can't find the words.

I put up a hand to silence him.

"We caught your guys on tape, Zero. But that's not what we're really mad about," I shrug. "See, you really fucked up. You sent one of your guys to murder our brother, Roman, while he was working. But you weren't successful, so then your men kidnapped and attempted to torture our woman. You weren't successful with that either, so then you targeted one of our drop sites. Nobody fucks with our brotherhood, nobody fucks with our business, and nobody fucks with our woman."

"I'm sorry, I—." He knows he's done, and it's not worth trying to articulate a feeble excuse.

"Repent in hell, you stupid fuck." Brick shoots Zero square between the eyes, blood and brain matter splattering on the family portrait behind his desk. "Bye, bitch," Brick grins and waves at the man's body. "Good riddance to a colossal waste of a carbon footprint."

We pick up the stolen haul that sits egregiously in the corner of Zero's office in a large cargo bag, and then walk out of the house the way we came, smoke still billowing in the hallway. The smoke reminds me of a technique I learned at culinary school. I might need to make barbecue sometime soon.

We head back down the hallway and down the stairs, out to the front of the compound. After stepping over countless bodies, we hop into our vehicle and drive home in silence.

Chapter Five

Aidan

Slade and Brick arrived back at the house a little earlier, both covered in blood and dust and grime. They tried to sit on the couch and tell me all about it, but I made them go take showers and change. Filthy fucks. I don't know what state this place would be in if I wasn't around.

It would probably look like a homicide scene in here, the amount of times we've all come back drenched in the blood of our enemies, streaked with dirt and mud and god knows what else. But that's par for the course when you're in the line of business that we are.

It's a relief to have Zero out of our lives. I knew that the two of them could take him down without my help. This wasn't one of those situations where three or four of us needed to go in guns blazing. He wasn't the strongest man on the island, but he had a decent-sized team and they were always trying to mess with our drops. Like a hundred noisy mosquitoes buzzing around your ears when you're trying to focus and be productive, always having to swat them away.

When Zero's guys tried to mess with Angel, I knew we needed to take care of him for good. When they messed with our drop, it seemed like the perfect time to address things all at once and put an end to him.

Now that he's out of our hair, we can focus on people with more power than us, and how we can take it from them, rather than stopping Zero and his men from trying to mess with ours. We need to focus on the bigger fish, not the annoying little minnows nipping at our ankles.

After they cleaned themselves up, Brick and Slade went out to run a few errands, and I'm waiting for them to come back and tell me more about what went down. I'm sitting in the living room absentmindedly flicking through TV channels. My mind drifts to what we observed earlier in Roman's room. I wasn't jealous when I saw Angel snuggled up against Roman, but it made me realize how much I want that for myself. She seems to trust me, at least more than she did at the start, but I feel like I need to show her how much I care about her.

If I can be the one who finds her stalker and helps to end her pain, I think it will show her how much I want her around.

My phone beeps and I look to see who's reaching out.

Anonymous: I know about the girl.

Aidan: Who is this?

I don't normally have time for anonymous texts, but anything that might be about Angel is, of course, going to pique my interest. Assuming that's the 'girl' the message is referencing.

Anonymous: That's not your concern. I believe she goes by Angel now, but that's not her real name.

Aidan: Wtf, who is this?

Okay, this *is* definitely about Angel. And this person seems to know about her past. She's been pretty up front, but we've only heard things from her perspective. I think she was telling the truth about everything, but what if there's more to it?

Anonymous: I have much to share. Meet me at the park beside 14 Palm Street. Don't tell your friends and definitely don't tell the girl.

Aidan: You've got to give me more info than that, man. It sounds like I'd be walking into a trap. What would I need to learn about her from you?

Anonymous: Do you want information on the girl or not?

Aidan: What kind of information?

Anonymous: Trust me, it'll change your mind about her.

Aidan: Trust an anonymous tester? Good one, bro. Go fuck yourself.

What kind of information could this person possibly have? Hearing it will change my mind about her is concerning, though. I'm certain this person is playing with me, but why is there a little voice in the back of my head saying I should find out more?

Anonymous: She'll destroy everything you ever worked for. You need to hear this.

Aidan: How do I know you're for real?

What if she's done this before? What if she's capable of ruining everything we've worked so hard for? Ugh, why am I letting an anonymous texter needle me like this? I'm losing my mind. But this might be important information, and I need to protect the guys.

Anonymous: Let me put it this way. If you don't meet me, I'm going to call the cops and let them know that you're harboring a captive. I'll also let them know about the not-so-little blood puddle I found on the floor of the salon.

Shit. I'm pretty sure we can figure the part out about the captive, assuming Angel would have our back and deny that's what was going on. And I think we did a reasonable job of cleaning up the evidence in the salon.

And what if we really can't trust Angel? What if she said we really were holding her captive against her will and corroborated witnessing Roman murder someone at the salon? The last thing we need is Roman in prison for homicide. It would be such a waste and would definitely tank our plans. I feel sick. We've worked way too hard to be taken down by something like this.

Aidan: I don't know who you are, and I don't know what you're talking about.

Anonymous: Meet me as instructed, and all will become clear.

There are clearly many things that are off about this exchange. I don't trust whoever this is for a minute.

It might be our only opportunity to get some background on Angel from someone other than her, and we need as much info as possible to track down her stalker, and also to figure out what to do with her after we catch him. But this sounds like a trap, and not one that I'm willing to fall for.

Yes, there's a chance she made up her entire story, and she's not the innocent woman she claims to be. She could be the one tormenting other people, but that seems unlikely. She seems really authentic and vulnerable, but you can't be too careful around people. There's always someone trying to fuck you over. Maybe she's not the exception I thought she was.

God, I'm sounding like Slade, all cynical and mistrusting. But that's what's kept us alive and able to build our empire so far. If we took everyone at their word, we'd all be under the dirt by now.

But who was she before she created her life on this island, before she created this new Angel identity? I need to know, and soon. This might be our only chance, and it's going to have a big impact on her fate.

This still feels like a trap, though.

And I guess this could be her stalker taunting me if everything she said was actually true. In which case, maybe he's volunteering himself to me. Part of me thinks I need to take whoever this is up on their offer so I can at least find out.

If it is him, we already know he's going to pay for everything he did to her, and everything he put her through. And this might just bring us one step closer to finding him and doing what we need to do before he has any hope of touching her again.

No, that's silly. This is clearly a trap. I don't fall for traps that easily.

I'm so conflicted. I should just leave it alone.

We're going to find him without needing to engage in whatever this is.

A couple of minutes later, my phone beeps again. This time it's from Brick's number. Which is a bit weird, because Brick isn't much of a texter. Prefers 'old fashioned voice conversations', he says. Enjoys hearing the sound of his own voice, more like it. Likes to talk on the phone and tell stories while he gets to the point. But I guess he does text from time to time, so it's not completely unheard of.

Brick's phone: Hey man, I got a text from an anonymous number and they have information on Angel.

Aidan: So did I. I'm pretty sure it's a trap.

This anonymous texter must be doing the rounds. Makes them seem desperate, trying to find the weakest link. Or maybe they're just thorough. I'm not sure which, but either way I don't like it.

Brick's phone: I need to follow the clues. I'm going to meet the person.

Aidan: The fuck you are. Stay away. Come back to the house.

Brick's phone: Sorry, man. I can't pass up this opportunity to learn more.

Aidan: Listen, what have I told you about being impulsive? And how it puts us all at risk?

He's always like this. Never vets things out properly. Acts and reacts without thinking through any of the consequences. It's going to bite us in the ass one day... it already has a few times, but luckily, the impact has been fairly minimal. But the stakes are getting higher, and it could only take one wrong move to lose all we've worked so hard for.

Brick's phone: Well, then talk to Slade. He's already gone to meet her.

Aidan: Excuse me, what did you just say?

Brick's phone: Yeah, I told him to wait for me, but he was anxious to find out more about Angel.

Aidan: Of course he was. He's been trying to find out anything bad about her from the start. When did he leave? Where did he go?

I am fuming. Slade… the most risk-averse human I know, always seeing the worst in anything. But when he has a bone to pick with someone, when something might validate one of his conspiracy theories, he's suddenly almost as reckless and impulsive as Brick.

In this case, of course Slade would have been the first to respond. He's been aching to find out something bad about Angel. Searching for it, needing it, to prove she's some kind of terrible person. If this really is a trap, which I'm realizing it almost certainly is, he is their prime target. Putty in their hands. If whoever this is doesn't get to him first, I'm going to teach him a lesson after this.

Brick's phone: He said something about Palm Street. Which is the same address the number texted me about.

*Aidan:		For fuck's sake. Why did he go alone? That's stupid.*

Brick's phone: I don't know what to tell you. But I'm going to go meet him now. You should come, too.

*Aidan:		Don't tell me Roman went as well.*

Brick's phone: No, but bring him with you. It can be a party.

*Aidan:		Brick, just wait for me, please. I'll come meet you somewhere and we can go together.*

Brick's phone: There's no time, man. I need to know more now. If you want to join me, come meet me over there.

Aidan: Brick, just wait, please.

Brick's phone: No time, sorry Aidan.

I try calling Brick's phone, thinking maybe hearing my voice will get through to him, but it goes straight to voicemail. Fuck, these guys just don't listen sometimes. Their habit of wanting to rush in and fix things without thinking them through has put us in countless dangerous situations. Generally, I'm able to talk some sense into them, but now and then they can't be stopped.

Then again, I also almost went racing to this address to meet this anonymous texter and find out information about Angel. If I was about to be that impulsive, Slade and Brick didn't stand a chance.

I feel a little tingle at the base of my neck. It usually happens when my subconscious senses that something seems a bit off. Brick's texts sounded like him or the most part, I guess, but his writing was maybe a little more precise than normal. Or maybe I'm reading too much into it. I'm on high alert with everything going on, and I'm infuriated that Slade would go off without either of us, and that Brick would follow behind. I'm looking for something, anything, that can explain the insanity of what's happening right now.

Against my better judgement, I'm going to go and meet them. I hope they're both okay. I'm pretty certain this is a trap. Who it's a trap for, and who built the trap, remains to be seen.

***

After a twenty-or-so-minute drive in my SUV, I roll up to Palm Street, which, like the name suggests, is lined with tall palm trees as well as carefully curated hibiscus and plumeria trees and other landscaped greenery. A few cars are parked on the sidewalk, and remnants of kids' activities are strewn about in the form of forgotten toys and basketballs lying in gutters and on the curb.

It's a quiet suburban area, almost like a cul-de-sac in terms of nothing interesting happening except for Tupperware parties and kids running around playing ball on the street. But instead of it being a dead end, there are quiet intersections at either end, and the odd vehicle will rumble by at sporadic intervals. Seems like a strange choice to meet someone with intel on Angel, but it's the only option I feel I have right now. Plus, I need to find these idiots and make sure they don't do anything stupid.

I glance around for signs of life. The homes are fairly quiet, with just the gentle sounds of people rousing from their slumber and making breakfast. Through open windows, I hear dulled notes of conversation and the occasional clanging of cooking utensils. In a few of the houses, I see people gathered around kitchen counters and dining tables. Do people actually make pancakes and bacon and eggs for their kids like on TV? Must be nice. Not the childhood I experienced. Growing up, I was lucky to get a knuckle sandwich for breakfast from most of my stepdads.

Where the fuck are these assholes? They're probably wandering around together laughing at how they got here before me. How they'll get credit for finding out info about Angel first. Or maybe I'll find them tied up somewhere and I'll have to rescue them. Ugh. Brick is so fucking heavy, I've had to drag him across the room before and it sucked all the energy out of me. I'm not looking forward to that, if that's the case.

"Aidan." A deep voice emerges from near me. I turn to my right to look, expecting to see Brick, and all of a sudden my brain reverberates in my skull. I put my fists up defensively, but it's too late. What the fuck. I'm a good fighter, but I just got sucker punched. This is so embarrassing. Everything is fading to black and I fucking deserve it.

Chapter Six

Angel

I'm pottering around my room, straightening things up. The guys all seem to be out doing something or other. When they get back, I'm looking forward to just relaxing with them. It's been so hectic around here and I just want some quiet time, to get to just enjoy their company. Of course, if that leads to other things, I will not complain. There are perks to living with four hot men, after all, and I intend to enjoy every one of them while it lasts.

My phone beeps. Oh, that sound is so refreshing. It's nice to have a phone again, to be trusted. I'm following Aidan's rules and I haven't reached out to anyone I know. I know that this is a dangerous time, and the last thing I need is to be tracked down by my stalker because I texted a friend here on the island. Besides, I don't want to put any of them in danger. And this phone is new, with only the guys' numbers in it, and I'm staying off social media. Everything should be fine.

Grabbing the phone off my nightstand, I glance down and it's from Aidan. A little smile forms on my face. I love it when the guys text me to let me know they're thinking of me.

I check the message.

Aidan's phone: Angel, I need you to come look at this.

Angel: What is it?

This sounds interesting. He's never texted me to go meet him somewhere before.

Aidan's phone: I found some info on the guy that's looking for you. But don't tell the other guys.

Angel: But you tell them everything. I don't understand.

Aidan's phone: There's no time. I think we have what we need to stop him. And you're the only one I can trust with this info.

Angel: Really?

Aidan's phone: Yes. Can't wait to show you. Hurry!

Angel: Okay.

He follows up his latest message with an address not too far from here. I know the general area, partially residential and part commercial. He's so risk-averse, there must be a reason he doesn't want the other guys to know about whatever he's found. They seem to tell each other everything, but these are unusual circumstances and there's always a method to his madness, and I've grown to trust him, mostly.

I pull on my black bomber jacket and tuck my bright purple hair into a wool hat. Despite the heat, I also pull on some black jeans. I'm not in a disguise per se, but I don't need to stick out like a sore thumb. I won the bomber jacket by doing a ton of Pilates classes one month as part of a challenge, and I feel good when I wear it because it reminds me I can kick ass when I want to. I guess I feel cute and strong, and that's a pleasant feeling.

It's exciting, going to meet Aidan like this without the other guys being aware. I've been feeling like they have the inside scoop on everything, and I'm the last to know, the outsider. So having Aidan reach out and confide in me like this, our own special time together, makes me feel a little giddy. Maybe the tables really are turning. Maybe I'm in the inner circle now, and more than just a captive, they don't know quite what to do with.

Okay, I'm probably delusional. It was just a text. Calm down, Angel, for fuck's sake. Sometimes someone says one thing with a hint of possibility and my mind spins it into a whole narrative where I'm at the center. The queen. Ridiculous.

As I walk toward the address Aidan sent through, I realize there's a lot to think about in terms of my future. I don't want to get ahead of myself. The guys are only keeping me around out of some sense of obligation, some feeling that they need to protect me, to defend me, from the evil psycho who has tormented me for more than half of my life. With their help, I think we have a chance to take him down and end his reign of torment once and for all. But once the threat is over, and it sounds like it will be soon, the guys may not see any reason for me to stay around. I'll just be back to what they saw me as in the first place. The witness to a murder that one of them committed. That doesn't bode well for me. I'll be a loose end again, and we know Aidan prefers dead ends to loose ends.

Even if they showed me some mercy and let me back out into the world, I don't know where I'd go. I'm assuming that they wouldn't want me staying around here, knowing what I know and having seen what I've seen. I created this island life to escape from the psycho. There's nothing left for me back on the mainland. He destroyed any remnant of that. If I went back, I'd have to reinvent myself again, in another town, under another name where my past couldn't follow me around. The thought of it is exhausting.

Cultivating new ties, making excuses why I haven't established a solid work history or credit, inventing a solid back story, knowing nobody and then meeting people who I can't tell shit.

On the very slim chance that they didn't banish me from here, I guess I could stay on the island and continue the life I've been building since I got here.

I enjoy running the salon, and the island is gorgeous.

The surfing is amazing, and the lifestyle is relaxed, except for the whole murder aspect.

One step at a time, though.

We have a psycho to destroy before I can start thinking of the possibilities, whatever they may be.

Chapter Seven

Angel

Following my phone's map directions, it takes me about half an hour to get to the neighborhood of the address Aidan sent through. On my way there, I spend the time thinking about how much has gone on since I met the guys, and wondering why Aidan wants me to meet him here. It's exciting to get out of the house, but I can't shrug off a sense of unease. I attribute it to wondering what happens after we take my psycho down, after I finally get to stop running from him.

As I head down the street lined with rows of tall palm trees, I hear a rustling behind me. I glance over my shoulder, but see nothing out of place. Shrugging, I turn back around. I need to get to Aidan, and he's probably impatient that I've already taken so long to get to him. But I walked fast and was trying to be sensible, not taking an Uber from the compound or anything like that which would leave a trail.

I hear another rustling noise behind me and turn again. This time, a shadowy figure steps out from a nearby tree and darts toward me. I try to run, but the figure moves too quickly, and suddenly they're right next to me. I cry out as I feel a sharp prick in my arm. And then everything goes black.

***

I wake to a bright light shining directly in my eyes. I squint and try to shade them with one of my hands, but my arms are not cooperating. I can't lift them at all, and I realize I'm tied down to the surface I'm laying on. It feels cold and smooth underneath me, my shoulder blades digging into what feels like metal. I try to move my legs, but they won't budge either. I look down, still squinting, and see they're bound at the ankles, too. I writhe around, trying to free myself, but the bonds are tightly secured. Where am I? How did I get here?

The room is clinical, with white walls, and some generic paintings hung on them. Stainless steel counters sit flush against each wall, the perfect place to set out sterilized tools and medications. I don't know where I am or exactly what type of facility this is. It could be a hospital of some sort, or maybe even a laboratory or scientific research facility.

Then I hear the cruel laugh, and it instantly sends an icy shiver down my spine. The unmistakable sound of Brett Wolf, my very own psycho stalker. I've blocked his name out of my mind, but with him in the same room as me, I'm finally letting myself think it. Not just Brett, never Mr. Wolf, always both names at the same time.

Brett Wolf, the man who tormented me for years, bringing out my darkness, leaving his horrific marks all over my body and my mind. Brett Wolf, the man who has never let me go, over the almost multiple decades he's festered in prison, thinking about me, obsessing, waiting to hunt me again. Brett Wolf, finding a way to get out of prison much earlier than expected and tracking me down on this island despite my efforts to bury my old self and start anew. His name, long blocked from my mind, now perforates every synapse in my brain, flooding all my senses. *Brett Wolf. Brett Wolf. Brett Wolf.* And now he's found me.

"Oh hello, there! You're awake. That's just... *perfect*," he whispers, almost theatrically. Even his whispers are full of excitement when he's doing something evil. I remember them well. "I've been waiting for you for seventeen whole years, but these few hours, while you were passed out, were the hardest by far." He paces around me, his gaze never breaking from being locked on me.

I shiver uncomfortably under his stare, trying to avoid direct eye contact, but it doesn't make a difference. I can still feel his eyes on me.

"I was so tempted to get started early, but I reminded myself that I needed to be patient. I enjoyed knowing I could do things to you while you were unconscious, like I used to, but the greatest pleasure has always been in making sure you're fully aware of what's about to take place. I had to hold myself back earlier, knowing that waiting for you to wake up will bring me the most enjoyment with what's about to happen."

His thin lips twist in what I can only imagine he thinks is a smile, even though it's the stuff of nightmares, revealing his chiclet-like teeth and the tip of his creepy pointy tongue.

He's really let himself go over the years he withered in prison. His skin is mottled and drab, likely no access to the expensive skincare products he was accustomed to on the outside. I can't believe I ever found him attractive. But I guess seventeen years of prison and being an evil maniac will do that to you.

I guess sometimes people are ugly on the inside and it eventually soaks through to the outside. It doesn't happen to everyone, but it has happened to him. He was always so proud of his appearance, and he's probably still better-looking than a lot of men his age. But I know he must hate looking in the mirror, and he must despise what he's aesthetically become. A minor victory, I suppose.

His body is still muscular, and he's much bigger than me. I'm sure he continued to work out throughout his time on the inside, determined to maintain his physical strength so he can continue to exert dominance over people weaker than him. He probably sees his physical upkeep as a testament to his mental vigor, something that he could still control from the inside when he had little control over anything else.

I shiver as his gaze runs over my body. "You still look like an angel when you sleep, you know," he says, his mouth hinting at another warped smile.
"I found it curious that you chose the name Angel when you attempted to hide from me, to start a new life. Like you were almost teasing me by pretending you wanted to start anew. Naming yourself something that I used to call you. It's almost like a special signal to me, a gift to let me know you were thinking of me. That you didn't really want me to stay away."

I want to vomit in my mouth. Gross. That is not at all why I chose the name. But now it makes me sick I didn't connect the dots at the time I picked something. I must have blocked out that he used to call me that as he inflicted wounds all over my body, typically while I was in and out of consciousness. Fuck, maybe I really do need more therapy.

"You've really been thinking about me this whole time? You couldn't find someone else to obsess over?" I narrow my eyes at him because that's all I can physically do right now. I wish my eyes could throw poison darts into his stupid body. I hope he feels my hatred as viscerally as I do.

"There's nobody else worth this level of focus, this dedication," he says softly. "You are my masterpiece. The work I am most proud of." His voice is surgical and precise, like everything he does. "Everyone before you was just practice."

I shiver. I knew I wasn't the first, and I'm not sure how many there were before me.

My Stockholm Syndrome was so bad for a while that I felt almost flattered that he saw me as being at the peak of his horrific acts. I was almost proud, almost felt special. I hated myself for those feelings, and they still make me feel very uncomfortable.

I shiver as he caresses my jaw with his hand. His fingers are long, but they're no longer nicely manicured, like they used to be. They're rugged, a little rough, no carefully buffed fingernails or neatly trimmed cuticles. He must have come straight to the island after being released, no time to refresh himself. He'd normally take the time to make sure everything was perfect and controlled. Maybe he's changed a little over the years, and he's not as prepared as usual. Maybe that's something I can use to my advantage.

My skin is crawling even after he removes his hand from my face, just like it always has since he started hurting me. To think at one time I was okay with, and even enjoyed, his touch. That didn't last long, but it still feels really creepy to know that at one point he made me tingle in a good way.

"And now I get to follow through on what I promised almost two decades ago. But now it's even better, because I've had so much solitary time to plan." He rubs his hands together and bounces from one foot to the other, jubilant. "Do you know what it's like to be completely solitary, *Angel*?" He laughs, more than a little unhinged. "It still sounds so funny to me, calling you that. Do you mind if I call you by your real name?"

He peers at me with one eyebrow arched, as if genuinely asking my permission. It makes one of his eyes look almost comically bigger than the other. His eyebrows are no longer neatly manicured like they used to be, but it's almost an improvement because he used to overdo it.

God, I'm tied down by my arms and legs, about to be tortured, and I'm critiquing this asshole's appearance. But he looks so different and yet the same, and it's the small things sometimes that keep us on the brink of sanity.

"Angel *is* my real name." There's no way I'm letting him call me by the other name. It's taken me a long time to get used to the new one, and hearing him call me by the other one might take me back *there*. I can't let him. I'm glad he didn't just automatically start, that he's almost deferring to me on this one thing.

"No, it's not, and we both know it. It might slip out. Sorry in advance." He winks at me, badly. He never could wink properly, something that probably really got to him. A weakness, the inability to wink, even if not useful. "Anyway, it's just a name, and I've always enjoyed calling you Angel while I worked on you. So I'll humor you for now, but apologies in advance if I accidentally slip back into old habits." He shrugs like someone might shrug to a friend if they did something annoying but still kind of cute. I shiver again. He lost his mind a long time ago, and it's clear he still hasn't come close to finding it.

"I'm not that person anymore. You have no right to call me by that name anymore." I jut my chin out defiantly. This is a test. I'm telling him not to do something, and I want him to know I've changed. Will this be enough to send him even further over the edge? If so, I'm fucked. It would mean he's completely lost control and I don't know him anymore.

"That's where you're wrong, though," his voice takes on a huskier tone, but it's still measured and precise. Thank goodness. I might be able to unravel him on my time and take advantage when he finally snaps. I think that's the only way I have a chance of getting out of here. "You'll always be that person, *Angel*. You can't run from yourself. You know I'll always have a hold over you, that I know you better than you do. Don't kid yourself."

I shudder as I remember him thrusting himself into me against my will, screaming my old name as if he truly believed I wanted it. The name that I can't bear to write or speak out loud anymore. That's what that name means to me now. Him, violating me against my will. Allowing other people to violate me. Hearing them say it out loud when they were ravaging my body, while I was trying to block out their grunts and groans and think of something else, anything else. Hoping they didn't snuff me out in the course of their perverted excitement.

I still can't quite believe I made it out alive back then. Sometimes I wonder if this is all just some kind of purgatory, that I really died and the universe doesn't know what to do with me.

His voice rips me from my thoughts. "You can run, you can change your name. You can call yourself Angel or Barbie or the Easter Bunny. You can pretend to be whoever you want. But it's all a facade." He grins at me again, his sharp incisors sticking out like fangs against the smaller nubs that line his evil mouth. "You're still a weak little girl who will succumb to my control and will. It's not your choice. You're just so damaged and unfixable. You always have been. Who cares what name you go by? It's your essence to be frail and vulnerable. Pitiful, really. I probably should have chosen somebody stronger to manipulate. More of a challenge than you."

He stares at me intently, his eyes overly bright. To me, he'd always had an intense gaze, but now I can see that it's fanatic, his emotions all tied to me. He lives to hurt me. His only goal is to destroy me in the most depraved way he can conjure in his sick, twisted mind.

But something has shifted within me, and this feels different from all the times he's tried to cut me down before. I'm so used to him telling me how weak and shitty of a person I am, that instead of decimating my self-esteem, instead of shredding me down to a husk of myself, his words now don't even scratch me. Instead, they make me feel sorry for him in a way.

It's been a while, but I've developed calluses in my soul, and I've become immune to those types of comments from him. I suppose the internal scars will never go away now. They're just there for all time, like my physical marks. But in this case, it's useful. My stomach isn't churning at his vitriol. I'm just enduring him and this moment. I can see through him, can finally see him for what he is.

How can I be his ultimate masterpiece if he really desires someone more challenging to manipulate? That makes no sense. He's gaslighting me, trying to diminish me with cheap shots. He hates me because he hates how obsessed with me he is. He hates that I make him lose control just by existing. That gives me power, and he doesn't know that I know it. But I do.

He peers at me more closely now, his eyes scrutinizing every inch of my face. "You have changed little, you know, Angel. You look just the same as when I last laid eyes on you in person seventeen years ago."

He circles around the table where I'm tied down.

"Must be the moisturizer I've been using. Keeps me looking young, just how you like us." I can't resist, even though I know he can't handle me being a smartass and it's going to cause me pain.

"Shut the fuck up! Don't you give me lip, you stupid little girl." He slaps me open-handed across my face.

It stings, but it was worth it. If I'm going to die, I'm going to piss him off in the process. Trust me, I'm not just going to lie here and take whatever he's trying to dish out on his terms.

"I've memorized every single detail, every single *pore* on your face, *Angel*. Every night, in my cell, I would dream of you. Of this day." A dreamy look spreads across his face, his mouth and eyes almost melting into his broader features. "And now it's here. I just want to savor it." The corner of one of his eyes tics a little, and he bites his lower lip as he continues to gaze at me. Jesus, if he keeps this up, he's going to come in his pants. I guess that's better than him trying to touch me, though. What a disgusting, evil monster.

"Haven't you tortured me enough?" I meet his gaze, and am pleased my face remains set in a scowl, no tremble giving away the residual fear I feel inside. "Don't you see that my body is already covered in scars because of you?"

His eyes trail down my body, as if he's admiring his own artwork through my clothing. "Oh yes, I remember how I inflicted every single one of them. To be honest, sometimes I jerk off to the memories of the ones I especially enjoyed creating." A grin spreads across his face and I swallow hard to keep the bile down that's threatening to exit my throat. "But that's just cosmetic. I know I've done far more to you than that."

"Yes, you fucking did!" I'm exasperated and I can't help my voice from rising. "You killed my soul! You made me dark inside!"

"Oh Angel darling, that's simply not true," he says, his voice dripping with condescension. "You give me far too much credit." He smiles a wicked little smile. "You had plenty of darkness within you already." He shrugs. "It's actually what drew me to you. I could see your... potential. And wasn't I right? Look at you now, trying to come across as so headstrong, but in reality very much still under my control."

"Fuck. You." I want to call him a psychopath, but I know he would just enjoy that. He's a lunatic. Unhinged, deranged, insane, obsessed with me. And he loves it. I do not.

"I wanted to haunt you in your dreams, you know," he says, nodding as he continues to study me. "I studied astral projection and lucid dreaming while I was in prison. My goal was to visit you every night, just to remind you I was there, waiting, biding my time until we could be together again."

Of course he would try to attack my dreams and my reality. Nothing is off limits for him, as if I'm not even allowed to nap without him trying to invade my inner thoughts. My brain conjured him up regardless, allowing my own sick version of him to haunt my dreams, my nightmares, and my every waking minute. So I guess he wins, even though he wasn't able to transcend dimensions and literally manipulate my dreams. And now here we are.

He pulls out a scalpel and twirls it gently so it sparkles under the light. He smiles as he admires the shimmering blade, and then turns his deranged grin to me. "Isn't this a beautiful tool? Worthy of being used on you, my dear Angel?"

I eye the scalpel as it glimmers. "Haven't you sliced me with one of those enough already?" I don't shrink away from the scalpel because he's used so many on me it may as well be a run-of-the-mill dinner fork or a butter knife. This fool has me desensitized to things that would have many people passing out from the fear.

"Oh, *Angel*, it's not the amount of times you do it. It's how much joy you get each time you do!" His voice booms with excitement, reverberating off the walls of the clinical room. "And I derive a lot of joy from slicing into your creamy flesh and leaving my mark on you. Mmm."

I shiver, my skin crawling as he describes marking me as his property. As I remember the slicing and singeing and the crispy burning odor as he branded my flesh. My blood, pouring from me, that he would scoop up in his hands and smear across his face and chest like some kind of war paint. That he would even drink it at times. The sick fuck.

"I suppose you're hoping those four men of yours will protect you, aren't you, Angel?" He peers at me as if he's trying to pick the best spot to slice me with the scalpel. "Not to be the moral police, but it seems slutty of you to be going around fucking four guys at once. Especially when they all live under the one roof."

I narrow my eyes at him again. It's about the worst I can do to him in my current predicament. "Oh, please stand there and continue to slut-shame me. Ironic, given you used to rape me and allow your rapey acquaintances to do the same. That's what you were doing, you know. That's what it called when you perform sexual acts on someone against their will."

His face darkens for a moment, and I think he's going to deny it, to insist that I wanted all those things to happen. But just as quickly, it returns to normal and goes back to his current version of 'normal'.

"Oh, I think I hit a nerve," he grins. "I'll be hitting more of those later when I bring out some of my other tools. This is going to be such a fun evening, for me at least." He rubs his hands together again with anticipatory glee. "I hope you get some enjoyment out of it too, *Angel*. This should be enjoyable for you as well."

I glare at him, adjusting my shoulders against the metal surface below me to try and get more comfortable. "You don't need to keep saying my name like that. And you never cared much for ensuring anything was enjoyable for me, so please don't feel the need to start now."

"I don't *need* to do a lot of things, *Angel*, but I choose to." He shrugs. "As I was saying, your friends won't be able to save you because I sent them on a wild goose chase. Similar to how I lured you here." He smirks, clearly proud of himself.

"Wait, the guys? What have you done to them?" A lump instantly forms in the pit of my stomach. This was my biggest fear. Forget what plans he has for me and what he ultimately ends up doing to my body. I'm concerned about the guys being brought into this. I know they're big and strong and can handle themselves against some terrifying people, but this is my psycho stalker and I don't need him interacting with the only good part of my life right now. This is my battle to face.

"Oh, I cloned their phones," he grins, looking very proud of himself. "Your little Aidan was so worried about you. He didn't come to me at first, but I told him little Bricky-dicky and Sladey-wadey were on their way to me, and he fell for it hook, line and sinker. And as for them, well, I led them to believe you were somewhere else on the island. They should be just about as far from here as they possibly could be without leaving the shore."

My heart sinks. "What did you do to Aidan?"

"Oh, you're worried that I hurt your boy? How... sweet of you. I must say, I'm a little jealous that you care about someone other than me. I'm going to take it out on him as soon as I'm done with you."

He's said too much. His little slip just now means Aidan is alive. A wave of relief washes over me as I realize he's prioritizing destroying me over ending the lives of the men I care about so much.

"Anyway, I'm sick of talking about them," he says, his eyes narrowing. "I want to talk about you, Angel, and how I'm going to separate your body into tiny little pieces while you're still alive. How I'm going to savor every moment as I destroy you after all these years. Mmm, this is going to be my best work yet."

"Whatever." I roll my eyes at him. "It's not like there's anything you haven't done to me before already. Do your worst."

He glares at me, and I see him ball one of his hands up in frustration. But this time, he resists the urge to hit me.

"Come on, Angel, please," he says, his eyes pleading with me. "This isn't how I imagined it. It's not how it's meant to go." His voice is almost whiney, like a little rich kid having a tantrum because he didn't get his full allowance or because not all of his friends showed up at his party. Pathetic. "It's not as much fun torturing someone when they don't care whether they live or die. I prefer it when they struggle. I like to see the fear in their eyes. The situations where they start off trying to be heroic, to save their own life. Where they summon their strength and give it their all, and then I get to see the light extinguish from their eyes. The moment they figure out they're not good enough, that they're not powerful at all, and that they're going to die and there's nothing they can do about it."

"So, you get off on human suffering? That's hardly a shocker. I mean, look what you did to me." I gesture at my body. "Haven't you done enough already? You've hurt me so much that you've made me numb. I'm like a drug addict that can't get high anymore.

You've made my resistance super strong. I'm completely desensitized at this point. If you don't like my lack of reaction, you only have yourself to blame."

"Oh, I still have plenty of ways to hurt you," he growls. "And I'm going to do something I haven't done before. I'm going to destroy your face. I can't wait to take away your beauty. It's the one thing I've preserved this whole time, the one line I didn't cross. I've never touched your face."

He moves to the side of the room and picks up a vial of something that's bubbling despite no apparent heat source. Is that acid? Jesus. He twirls it in his hands. "I'm going to wait to use this, although I've fantasized about it for a very long time. Watching your flesh disintegrate, making you into a grotesque creature that only I could love. Your men will think you're hideous once you're all melted. It's going to be wonderful when I'm the only one who'll even be able to bear looking at you."

"That's it? You want to make me ugly? That's your major goal? Good one." I roll my eyes, even though I'm terrified of acid chewing at my flesh. That really would be a new form of torture, and one that I won't be able to hide with long sleeves or pants.

"Beauty is pain, *Angel*," he shrugs. "And you're my most beautiful masterpiece." He smiles at me again, his hideous teeth bared. I shiver, and I'm feeling actual fear at this point. He's reaching new lows, extra levels of crazy. He's threatening me with actions that can't be undone, and ones that I might not survive.

Fuck.

"So, while they're off hunting you down on the other side of the city, we're going to have our own little fun and pick up right where we left off all those years ago." He puts the vial down for now, thank goodness, and returns to my side.

He caresses my jaw again and I try to move my face away, but he holds it in place, controlling me like always. God, I desperately want to vomit all over him, but I need to remain calm and pretend to be doing what he says while I figure out how to escape. He continues muttering about our time together before he killed my family and all my friends. How much I mean to him, how much he enjoyed causing me unbelievable pain. He's so repetitive that I tune him out, even though his words are completely insane.

One thing is clear. He's even more deranged than the last time I saw him. Seventeen years on the inside have not treated him well in terms of his mental health.

He's so busy taking a trip down memory lane that he doesn't notice me squeezing my right wrist ever so slightly, trying to slip it through my restraint, or at least loosen it. I'm determined to get out of here, even if I get injured in the process. Better off injured than dead. I don't even care if he disfigures me at this point, as long as I leave here alive.

"Your family couldn't protect you," he sneers. "Honestly, I don't think they cared about you enough or they would have figured out a way. It's a bit sad, really, having a family that doesn't care enough to save you." There he goes again with his hurtful comments. "And now neither can these men." He shrugs. "It's a bit of a pattern you've got going for you, isn't it, *Angel*? Everybody close to you seems to let you down. To leave you here on this plane to fend for yourself. It must make you wonder to yourself, is it something about you? Are you not somebody worth sticking around for? Are you not capable of being protected because you're just so... broken and irreparable on the inside? It must make you feel sick, realizing that you're not somebody that's worth saving."

His words used to break me down, but now I just listen as he rattles off his psychobabble, trying to manipulate me into my old sorry state. This time, I see how he tries to slice me deeply with every word choice. He's physically holding an extremely sharp scalpel in his hand, but nothing could cut as deftly as his words. Using his knowledge of my family life against me. Preying on my vulnerabilities.

But instead of cowering and crying and thinking dark thoughts about my self-worth, I just let it all go. I forgive myself for falling for this bullshit in the past. I see him for all his manipulation, and how he's actually very skilled at it. Younger, more inexperienced me didn't stand a chance.

But he doesn't know who he's up against now.

What he doesn't realize is that I'm out here in this world now just trying to get by. Like we all are. But I don't have an anchor to guide me home. I'm rudderless. I'm my own anchor. And that's scary sometimes, not having a backstop. I look at all my friends and their family relationships. They might seem like a pain sometimes, like more trouble than they're worth—the obligations and feelings and baggage that come with them. But at the same time, they provide a foundation and roots and a place to go when the world is crumbling all around you. But in my case, I only have myself. And I do have my chosen family, but as I've learned, those relationships can come and go. There's not the same permanence that you find with a 'real' family. I am my own rock, and that's a big role to fill sometimes. I've been told I'm brave many times, but really, I'm out here just trying to exist. What he doesn't realize is that I'm done with his suffering. No matter what he does, he can't hurt me anymore. Not like he used to. And I don't have anybody centering me, making me weak. I thought my being anchorless was a weakness, but I've come to realize it's my ultimate strength. I have nothing and everything to live for.

His words have lost their power over me. But instead of letting on that he's not affecting me, I indulge him, playing along as if he's getting to me. Tears spring forth from my eyes and he looks pleased, because he thinks he's the cause, when really, it's the pain of squeezing out of one of the wrist restraints. I inch my hand along, folding it in on itself as much as I can, and I can feel that it's slick with blood, lubricating the restraint and assisting my hand along. I grimace, and he assumes it's in response to another of his stinging verbal attacks, but it's because my thumb feels like it's going to buckle in on itself as I squeeze it out of the restraint, leaving my hand loosely inside the fastening.

He's so enthralled by watching my reactions to his words, so consumed by my every micro-expression, that he fails to notice what's going on so close to him. He's so obsessed with me, with thinking that his words have such an emotional impact on me, that he misses what's right in front of his face.

"I love hurting you," he growls. "I love watching the way you are so weak against my words." He's clearly aroused, and I'm sure he's on the verge again of coming in his pants.

"Yes, stop hurting me, daddy." It slips out, and I want to vomit, but his eyes light up and I know I said the right thing to keep him distracted. He always loved it when I called him that. Let him think that's what this is about. Pleasing him, fulfilling his every desire, including ultimately destroying me. This sick fuck is going down, and he has absolutely no clue. I love it, and I'll be gross and say exactly what he wants to make it happen.

My fingers inch along above me until I feel them tap against a long, thin object. Ha! The fucking idiot placed a scalpel on the bed for later use, too busy luxuriating in his nostalgia. Too busy staring at the pores on my face to notice me escaping right under his eyes.

"Anyway," his eyes grow dark and a scowl forms on his face. It's the first negative emotion I've seen from him in a while. "I can't stop thinking about you and your four men. You stupid slut."

"Oh, for fuck's sake, Brett Wolf."

His eyes light up as he hears me say his name out loud.

"How is that any different from the men you forced on me for your entertainment?" I arch an eyebrow at him. " Or was it different because you were in control of that situation?"

His eyes grow darker. He's distracted, wild. I've hit a nerve. "What is it about these four guys, though?" His voice is whiney again. "They seem like vile human beings to me, *Angel*. If I had anything to do with it, they'd be dead. And that's exactly what I'm planning on as soon as I've finished with you. Ideally, I'd force you to watch as I slowly kill them one by one. But it's taken me seventeen years to get to you again, and I can't take any risks. Believe me, each one of them is going to die a slow and grisly death."

The scalpel is now firmly in my grasp, my wrist free. My heart is racing, and blood is pounding in my head. I can't stand to hear him talking about my men like this. Any fear that existed within my body has fled the scene. I'm breathing fast, adrenalin coursing through my veins. He's threatening my guys. I might not know what they will do to me after all this is said and done, but for now, they're all I have. And it's time to shut him up.

"Stop talking about my fucking family!" I scream and slash at him with my free hand. My use of the word 'family' to describe them isn't lost on me, but I'll process that later.

He jumps back and I use the scalpel to slash my other wrist to freedom, and quickly do the same for the ropes attached to my feet. I jump off the bench that I've been tied to throughout my time in this room, and wildly slash in his direction.

"You fucking bitch!" he screams, his voice hollow and raspy as he tries to stay just out of my reach. I'm out of control and so is he now, just like I know he hates. "This isn't meant to happen! You're meant to let me finish you, to let me take what you owe me."

"I owe you *nothing*!" I scream, blood slamming against my temples with force. I'm so worked up, so rageful, that I'm worried I might black out. "I have already given you *everything* and more! You took so much that didn't belong to you. There is nothing left to give you!"

Unfortunately, he regains his composure remarkably quickly as I scream at him, as if my 'acting out' makes him take on the condescending parental role once again.

"Now, *Angel*. I know this must be very difficult for you, taking a long, hard look at yourself. You're acting out of control. This is why you need my help." He shrugs, his voice once again oozing with condescension. "Why don't you just use the scalpel on yourself now? You could rid yourself of the darkness so easily. You know where to cut. I've shown you before. You have a few options... here, here and here." He gestures to the parts of the body that really shouldn't be sliced if you want to stay alive.

I ignore him, blood continuing to rush to my temples. A loud heavy metal song blares in my brain. I've learned to drown out his words with imaginary music, and it's kicking in as if I'm at a death metal concert. We circle the table where I was restrained just moments before. I hiss at him, chasing him, scalpel in hand. He jumps backwards, but again my wildness seems to calm him and he moves toward me.

Without warning, he leaps to the side and picks up another of his tools from one of the stainless steel counters. It's a longer, much sharper knife. There's no way that I can reach him with this much smaller scalpel when he's holding that thing. I try to circle around to the door to make an escape, figuring I can plot revenge later if only I can get out of here, but he realizes what I'm doing and he just laughs.

"Oh, *Angel*. How silly you must think I am. Falling for that? Do you think I would let you escape so easily after seventeen years of waiting to take what's mine?" He cackles, the same unhinged laughter that has haunted my nightmares for decades.

I feel my eyes narrow. An attempt to make him and his atrocities look smaller, maybe. "What the fuck is your problem? Why are you so obsessed with me? What is it about me?"

"Like I said, *Angel*. It's the darkness within you that attracted me to you in the first place. Seeing it pouring out of you energizes me. I dream of the times I used to cover myself in your blood. It was invigorating, energizing. And I'm so looking forward to drinking more of it tonight. The most I have ever consumed of you, my darling. There won't be a drop left by the time I'm done."

What a fucking nutter. I have to keep him talking while I figure out how to escape.

He leaps onto the restraint table. I don't even know how he gets up there, but it's an impressive athletic move. Maybe it's the adrenalin fueled by his obsession, but suddenly he's way too close to me with his sharp knife in hand. He hops down from the table on the side closest to me, no longer a barrier between us.

Now he's laughing, his eyes boring into me, as he corners me. There's nowhere to escape. For more than half my life, I've feared that I'd die at his hands. That I'd succumb to his psychopathic obsession, and he'd trap me in my darkness forever. And now that time has come.

I resign myself to my fate, but I'm determined to at least cut him a couple of times in the process. Inflict a bit of pain before he kills me. I'll fight until the last moment. That's a guarantee. I crouch into a staggered position the way I would on a surfboard, my center of gravity low, knowing that will afford me the most balance, and I lash out and slash one of his shins with the scalpel. The blade cuts through his flesh like butter and I feel it scrape against bone. He screams in agony, almost dropping the knife.

"You fucking bitch!" he cries out, his eyes narrowing and turning from dark brown to pitch black.

As he advances on me with the knife pointed toward my heart, I realize I'm probably going to die in the next minute. There's nowhere for me to run. He's bigger, his knife is bigger. I'll still fight, though. I won't give up. I can't give up.

He circles around me, still pinning me into the corner because of his hulking presence. He's blocking me from the door. Getting through that slab of wood is my only chance to stay alive, and he knows it. He advances on me, the blade only inches from my torso.

Suddenly, the door to the room flies open and a baseball bat smashes Brett Wolf in the head, sending him crumpling to the floor. I soon see that attached to the bat is Brick's large hand, and of course, the rest of Brick. He comes into full view, and so do Slade and Roman.

Slade runs to me on one side, Roman on the other, and they help me to my feet.

"Are you okay, Angel?" Slade asks, his eyes full of concern.

I can't form words. This is so much to process.

"Talk to us, Angel. Please," says Roman. "Are you alright?"

I try again to formulate words, but something's missing. Then it clicks. "Wait. Where's Aidan?"

"Brett Wolf smacked him on the back of the head and knocked him out," says Roman. "That's why you thought Aidan texted you. It was really this psychopathic piece of shit." He kicks at Brett Wolf with his foot. "I guess he cloned our phones and tricked Aidan, and then sent us messages saying you were somewhere completely different. We were able to track Aidan's phone and figure out where you were." He glances around. "It looks like we got here just in time."

I nod.

"Oh my god," I gasp. "Aidan...is he okay?"

"Yeah, the doctor was coming around to check him out. Should be there right now, actually. But based on our quick phone conversation, he seemed to think it was just a moderate concussion. Sounds like this asshole," he points his thumb toward Brett Wolf, "sucker punched him out of nowhere."

"As for this guy," Brick kicks Brick Wolf in the center of his back while he lies unconscious on the floor, "he's coming with us."

"What are we going to do with him?" My eyes are wide. I've been so resigned to him ending my life that I haven't even thought about what I might do if suddenly I gained control over him.

"It's pretty simple, really," says Slade, his eyes narrowing at the unconscious figure, finally scowling at someone who actually deserves it. "We're going to kill him, and we're going to make sure it hurts."

"We sure are," grins Brick, his eyes dreamy. "It's going to be a fitting performance. He's going to regret the day he ever met you, my Valkyrie. Nobody fucks with our queen and lives."

"What do you mean? How will you do it?"

"It's a bit of a case of choose your own adventure, really," says Brick, unusually cryptic. His gaze meets mine. "I need to ask you a very important question, Angel."

"Like what?" This is a weird time for Brick to be randomly quizzing me. But Brick is a kook, after all, so here we are.

"Like... what's his biggest fear?" His gaze is even more intense than usual. "Not just something he doesn't like. His actual biggest fear, the thing that he has nightmares about."

I think about it, and I've spent so many years fearing my stalker and what he's capable of that I've never really considered what he himself fears. Then again, I've spent a lot of time with him, and that's unfortunately lent itself to me getting to know him and his delusional mind well. After a moment of mulling it over, a lightbulb goes off in my mind, and I grin. It's so obvious.

"Not being in absolute control."

Brick nods, and then his face explodes into a broad grin. "Excellent. I have just the idea."

I feel a ripple of excitement. The thought of exacting revenge on the man who has made my life a living hell seems almost too good to be true. After hunting me, stalking me, abusing and torturing me, raping me, annihilating my entire family and everybody close to me, it felt like he was the unstoppable one.

Getting out of prison and coming straight after me was a bold move, but it only points to how unhinged he is, how he's been festering in his jail cell, thinking only of me. My skin crawls as I imagine him obsessing over what he wanted to do to me once he was out.

"You ready to go?" Slade asks, a rhetorical question clearly. Why would anyone want to stay around here after what just happened?

Without a word, Brick grabs Brett Wolf from underneath each of his arms and Slade grabs his legs. They carry him to the car and throw his bulky body into the trunk. As they toss him in, the impact causes him to rouse. His eyes slowly open, and he groans and gives Brick a questioning look. He attempts to prop himself up onto his forearms, but he can barely hold himself up.

"Oh haiiiii! I've heard you're quite the planner," Brick grins. "And that's such a lucky coincidence, because we have quite the plans for you! A win-win, if you will. A mutually satisfying exchange! I can't wait to show you what we've come up with! But now it's nap time, nighty night!"

In a familiar move that all the guys apparently know and love to use, Brick pulls a gun out of his holster, rears it up behind him and brings it down hard on the top of Brett Wolf's skull. He crumples back into the trunk, and Brick closes it with a satisfying click. "Baiiiii!"

Chapter Eight

Angel

I'm not sure what to expect when I get to the basement. The guys made me go upstairs to wait until they have everything ready, and now that I'm all set for whatever they have planned, every minute feels like hours. Standing around waiting to be called down has me on tenterhooks. I can't quite believe we've taken my captor captive, and not only do I get to live, I get to get revenge!

Brick told me to dress in my wildest outfit, to channel the most elaborate version of myself that feels most empowered and powerful. To wear what I believe will terrify Brett Wolf the most, and sear into his brain as the last thing he sees. *The last thing he sees.* It sounds so surreal, but it needs to happen. My brain is still processing. This is all so unbelievable, but it's actually happening. What a trip.

I've picked an all black outfit. Tightly fitted leggings, matte black, and a slightly sparkly corset that I've never had the courage to wear before. My tits look great in it, but that's for me, not for Brett Wolf.

My makeup is bold, and I extend the wings of my eyeliner far beyond where I normally would, dramatic and intense. My lashes are thick and dark, my lipstick a striking red. I did not come to play today.

For shits and giggles, I've adorned my back with fairy wings. It might be a bit extra, wearing wings, but Brick inspired me. If there's one thing he's taught me, it's not to be afraid to be my authentic self, no matter the cost. I've carried them around for years, always wondering if I'd get to the point I'd ever actually wear them. Today is that day. They stretch broadly behind me, making me look broader, bigger, more powerful. Ready for revenge.

Unusually, Brick also gives me a corsage to wear, promising me that today would be 'like the best prom you've never been to.' I shook my head and smirked at the time, but I've put it on over my wrist as instructed. It's a beautiful black rose that would make a nice tattoo now that I see it on my hand. He's so hot yet so fucking weird, but in a way that makes me feel like a princess. No, not a princess, an absolute queen.

Finally, after what seems like forever but was probably only about an hour, the guys call me down to the basement. I'm so ready, but still not sure entirely what to expect. I just need to trust. They know everything I've been through now, and I'm confident they'll have put a lot of thought into whatever they've come up with, especially Brick given the venue is his precious torture basement. Every little detail will have been accounted for, and all I need to do is show up.

I walk down the wooden steps that normally descend into darkness, but it looks and sounds a lot different today. The basement has been completely transformed. Instead of a clinical concrete room built for torture, it's now an insane, noisy, and colorful carnival of horrors.

Garish masks with mouths snarling in horror and torment cover the walls and hang from the ceilings.

Loud, disorienting music blares from surround sound speakers. Strobe lights dance across the walls, and flashing lights surround vintage funhouse signs. The high-pitched beeps of carnival games reverberate off the concrete walls, creating a wild cacophony of chaos.

There's a touch of fairytale madness down here, too. Black and white rabbits and playing cards and black-light and neon artworks featuring torture scenes and wild sex acts also adorn the walls. I'm guessing that Brick chose these, and I'm not going to question how he got hold of them so quickly. It's cluttered and loud and a barrage of disparate sensations, which I can immediately tell is exactly what it's intended to be. This place is designed specifically to disorient, to mess with your senses, and it's working in the best way.

There are even containers of freshly made popcorn, the salt and butter scent pervading the room, and cotton candy sitting on a stand off to the side, covered in real worms that slither over the contents.

It's hard to feel anything like control in a place like this. Brick has received the memo and has executed on the assignment. This stage of it, anyway. I can't wait to see what happens next.

"It's time!" Brick calls out, grinning broadly.

As if he's completing a regular errand, Slade casually wheels my psychotic stalker into the room on a cart, and with the help of Aidan and Brick, he secures him to shackles suspended from the ceiling. A piece of material tied tightly around his head gags Brett Wolf's mouth. Which is wonderful and surreal for me—someone has finally got him to shut the fuck up.

It's refreshing to be in the same room with him without hearing his unhinged laughter, his condescension, his attempts to make my entire psyche crumble from the slices of his cruel words. Now he's just a gagged man shackled to a ceiling. I love it.

Brick moves back into position behind a podium near the center of the room, right in front of where Brett Wolf is suspended from his shackles. He picks up a microphone. "Testing, testing, 1-2-3!" The microphone screeches and the sound quality improves, Brick's voice booming out of surround sound speakers.

He's wearing a blazer that's completely covered in multicolored sequins. It's loud and garish and fits right into this chaotic environment. He's lined his eyes with thick black eyeliner and drawn lipstick on his face in a manner reminiscent of a deranged clown. It's definitely crazy, but it suits him. He is just perfect. At this moment, I realize I love him so much. I have the urge to make out with him here and now, but we have more pressing matters and that can wait.

"Well hello there, Brett Wolf!" booms Brick. "Welcome to the island's newest game show, *All Your Dreams Come True!* I'd say 'come on down!' but you're already here!"

Brett Wolf jerks awake at the sound of Brick's game show host voice blaring from the speakers in the basement. He squints at the bright spotlight shining directly in his eyes. Ironic, considering that was my reaction when I woke up in the clinical room where he planned to torture *me* to death. The metal shackles connected to his wrists rattle and clank against the pipe above as he attempts to move his arms.

"No point in trying to struggle, Brett Wolf - we've got you safely secured for the duration of this game show! But I appreciate the enthusiasm!" Brick winks at Brett Wolf. "Wriggling around is futile and will just spend your valuable energy, which you're almost certainly going to need to be a worthy contestant and make it all the way to the end!"

He tries to kick his legs and flail about, but he's tied up so tightly that his toes and the balls of his feet barely graze the floor. "Now, now, we haven't reached the dancing stage of the evening, Brett Wolf. You're jumping the gun. It's best if you just stay still and await further instructions. Be patient!"

Brett Wolf groans and blinks repeatedly. He tries to adjust his posture in his restraints but doesn't have much luck. His shoulders adjust in resignation. He stills and sighs deeply, waiting for what's next.

Slade approaches him and undoes his gag, removing the fabric and revealing a bitter scowl. Brett Wolf coughs and splutters as he inhales deep breaths through his mouth.

"Now, tell us a bit about yourself, Brett Wolf! We like to get to know our contestants at the start of each show!" booms Brick. "We want to know what makes you tick! What do you like to do for fun?"

"I—who the fuck are you?" he growls, but his eyes are wide. I'm not used to seeing him scared. It's kind of fun, I could get used to this.

Recognition dawns on his face as he scrutinizes Brick more closely. His sparkly outfit clearly threw Brett Wolf off, which is fair. "Oh, you're one of those *men* that Angel has been fooling around with, aren't you?"

"It doesn't matter who I am, but I suggest you play along, Brett Wolf," Brick grins. "Because if you don't, there are going to be bonus prizes, and I'm not so sure that you'll like them."

Brett Wolf snarls, but that's about all he can do from where he's shackled. Who's the captive now? A little grin spreads involuntarily across my face. I just can't help it. I feel giddy with anticipation.

Brick pulls a scalpel out of his pocket and holds it up so that it glints off the bright lights in the basement. With the brightly colored carnival lights, there are glimmers of blue and red and yellow and green and purple. It's beautiful. "I warned you, buddy. Slade, will you hold the microphone for me while I do the honors?" Slade nods and Brick tosses him the microphone.

"As you can see, Brett Wolf here has earned himself the first bonus prize of the evening! And Brick here is going to administer it to him directly." Slade has a surprisingly legit game show host's voice as well, deep and resonant. I might suggest it to him as a backup career if this whole mafia-type gig doesn't work out, and I suppose if he can't become a chef, which is clearly what he was born to do.

Brick walks over and holds the scalpel in front of the spotlight so that it glints directly in Brett Wolf's eyes. He squints and flinches as Brick descends on him. Brick deftly slices off one sleeve of Brett Wolf's shirt, leaving his arm bare from the shoulder down.

Because Brett Wolf's shackles are suspended above him, the smooth, sensitive skin of his inner arm is exposed. Brick runs the scalpel along Brett Wolf's arm, from his armpit to his wrist, breaking the skin and carving so deeply that it takes a moment for the incision to bleed. It'll no doubt hurt like hell, but Brick made sure not to cut so deeply that my tormentor isI at any risk of bleeding out. I don't know exactly what the guys have planned, but I know we need this psycho to be conscious for the game show to work.

Brett Wolf's eyes grow wide and his nostrils flare as he stares at his bleeding arm. He screams in agony as the pain hits him, writhing as if trying to free his hand to hold in the blood and gore that Brick has just split wide open in his grotesque act of butchery. I'm sure he's not feeling the full extent of the deep gash, his body protecting him by partially throwing him into shock.

"I'm sorry if you're right-handed, Brett Wolf. You might have trouble signing your name for a little while!" Brick shrugs as if he's explaining something quite trivial. "Lots of tendons and other important things for motor function just got a little messed up there, bud."

The blood is trickling out of his arm in a steady stream. Not torrential, but enough to know that significant damage has been done. Sometimes deep cuts hurt so much that they stop hurting. You're just numb. But you still know they're there. It's the case for both physical and mental injuries. I'm not sure which is true for him right now, whether he's in agony or not. Either way, I know he's terrified. His breathing is fast and ragged. I sense him trying to regain control of it, but he can't. He must really hate this. Almost as much as I love seeing him like this.

"Now, are you ready to go back to playing the game, or would you like another bonus prize?" Slade raises an eyebrow in his direction.

Brett Wolf shakes his head, his face pale and covered in a light sheen.

"What was that?" Slade booms into the microphone. "I need to have a verbal answer from you for it to count. It's game show regulations, you see. Nodding and shaking your head doesn't cut it. We need audible acknowledgement. Would you like to play the game now, or would you prefer to take another bonus prize? Keep in mind the bonus prizes get bigger and better the further you advance in the game! Brick just gave you a little... slice... of what's to come, if you'll excuse the pun. Things will only get crazier from here on out!"

"P-play the game!" Brett Wolf stutters, saliva flying from his mouth. "Play... the gam e..." His voice trails off. It probably feels surreal for him too, calling out to continue this insanity.

"You got it!" Slade says, and Brick returns to take the microphone from him.

"Excellent, thank you for standing in there for me, partner." Brick high fives Slade, who steps back off to the side where the rest of us are standing, watching.

"Alright, so back to where we were," booms Brick. "Tell us a bit about yourself, Brett Wolf. What do you do for fun?"

"I—I don't know," he says, his eyes wide with panic, the whites showing around the entire iris.

"You'd better come up with something, Brett Wolf," Brick insists, his voice echoing off the concrete walls and only dampened by the plethora of garish carnival decorations adorning the space. "The clock is ticking! We need to know *all* about you if you want to survive this game!"

Brick presses a button on the podium and a chaotic, high-pitched tune plays, accompanied by a loud *tick-tock! tick-tock!* sound.

Brett Wolf's eyes dart around wildly, and then finally settle on Brick. He clenches them tightly shut, and yells, "Photography!"

"Excellent! Brett Wolf has selected photography as his first category!"

We all turn to Brett Wolf and applaud enthusiastically, as if his 'choice' of category is truly exceptional. He doesn't look so sure, his eyes bugging as the sound of our synchronized claps reverberates off the walls just like Brick's voice.

"Now our co-host, who I believe you may know, is going to ask you some questions and put you to the test to see if you can make it through to the next stage. Come on down, co-host! My beautiful Valkyrie, or as you may know her, Angel!" Brick makes a flourishing gesture to welcome me onto our 'set'.

I step from the shadows into the spotlight so that I'm silhouetted in front of it, and I curtsy flamboyantly to my left and then to my right as the guys all clap loudly for me.

Brick reaches over and hands the microphone to me, as well as a stack of cue cards. Noticing my reflection in one of the basement's many shiny carnival games, I can see I really am wearing an outfit inspired by a Valkyrie. I knew Brick would like my choice, and it seems fitting for the occasion. An Angel of Death. That's what I am today. I added a few extra touches to my outfit right before I came down. My face is now painted with stripes that run from below my eyes, halfway down my cheeks. I added more black eyeliner so that it sweeps out and up even further, making my eyes look extra intense and dramatic and wild. The wings flare out broadly, and they twinkle under the wildly colorful lights that surround the basement space. The ensemble makes me feel powerful, confident, ready for the war we're waging today. Exactly how Brick intended for me to feel down here. I'm here to face my demons, and for once, I have the upper hand.

Brett Wolf squints, trying to figure out who I am, to make out my features. For a moment, it frustrates me he doesn't immediately guess it's me, but after all, he's always claimed to believe I'm weak, and right now I'm definitely in a position of power over him. He's not used to seeing me move confidently like this. He's not used to seeing me thrive in my element. I move closer to him to give his eyes a chance to adjust and take in the entire spectacle.

I want him to soak in every inch of me right now, to remember what he tried to create and to see instead how I've transformed into something far stronger than he ever imagined. Sometimes life is cyclical. Sometimes when you turn light into darkness, that darkness grows more powerful and ends up ultimately destroying you. I guess he took that risk and lost, and now is his day to pay the price.

"A-angel?" he snarls and narrows his eyes, his tone condescending despite his predicament. "Let me down or you'll regret it." I can't believe he's shackled to the ceiling with four men in the room who are determined to end his life, and he still has the audacity to threaten me. Actually, on second thought, I can believe it.

"Always so controlling. Always making me believe you're in the power position. Even when it's clearly a lie, like right now." My voice is firm and unwavering. I circle him, and on my way past his calf muscles, I kick one with the point of my shoe so that his wrists wiggle in the air above him. He jerks awkwardly, swaying in the air before coming to a complete stop.

When I'm satisfied he's not moving anymore, I finish my circling and stand in front of him again.

"So for your first round, the topic is photography, by your choosing," I say calmly. "Now tell us, Brett Wolf, what type of photography do you like to do?"

He lowers his brow and blinks rapidly, his eyes wide each time he opens them.

"The clock is ticking!" Brick says, leaning over so the microphone picks up his voice. "No time for dilly-dallying, contestant number one!" He plays the high-pitched carnival tune with the accompanying *tick-tock!* sound again. It echoes wildly off the walls, and Brett Wolf clamps his eyes closed as if trying to will a palatable answer into his mind. Or maybe he's trying to will himself away from this madness.

He blinks rapidly again. "Flowers!" he yells.

"Oh yeah? Flowers, you say? What kind of flowers?" I ask, arching an eyebrow and smirking at him. This man doesn't know shit about flowers, and he knows I know it. "I didn't pick you for a florist, Brett Wolf! Where did you develop your interest in flowers? And what types of flowers float your boat?"

"I don't know," he groans meekly, sweating under the harsh spotlight. "Any growing in the garden, I suppose. Wherever I see them. Colorful ones with leaves!"

I flip over the cue card in my hand. "I'm afraid that's the wrong answer, Brett Wolf! Honesty is a very important part of this game."

The guys standing behind me nod and murmur, "Very important."

"We're going to need you to fess up to your real preferred type of photography. Or otherwise Brick's going to give you another bonus prize. The more honest you are in this game, the more likely you are to live. Simple stuff, really."

Brick grins at Brett Wolf, probably hoping Brett Wolf is going to tell another lie so Brick can have some more fun with him.

"Okay—okay!" Brett Wolf pants, on the verge of hyperventilation. The balls of his feet each slip out from under him, one after the other, as he tries to gain balance, making him jerk awkwardly underneath his shackles.

He eventually regains his footing. His skin is flushed, and his eyes dart from me to the shadows where he knows the men are standing and watching, ready to jump in. But then, he seems to solely focus on me, and he gets the look in his eye that causes a shiver to jolt down my spine. The look he used to give me when I was under his spell. He's regaining control, figuring out how to fixate on his obsession despite all the noisy and colorful distractions around us.

"I like to take pictures of sluts like you," he growls, then spits in my direction. "Ugly loser whores who are so thirsty for a man. You're so gross. No man would ever want you."

"Oh okay," I nod. I hear Slade growl in the corner. "Thank you for the feedback. Anything else?"

"You weren't a virgin when I met you. You were spoiled. You are a disgusting mess that nobody would ever want. You're destroyed. Your parents don't even like you and wish you were never born."

"Okay then. Thanks again. Keep going." My voice is calm and steady, which just serves to agitate him more. Which is exactly what I want to happen.

"You're insecure and your tits are too small. Your ass is so fucking gross."

Slade growls again, and out of the corner of my eye, I see Aidan holding him back.

I nod. "Okay, thank you for all of your valuable input. I appreciate your transparency and candor." I resist the urge to roll my eyes.

I turn and walk toward Brick, but then change my mind, flip back around and walk back up to Brett Wolf.

"I have another question for you. Why are you so obsessed with me?" I peer at him and laugh, scrunching my shoulders up and grinning at him side-on, letting out a loud and crazy giggle that echoes off the basement walls like a creepy doll come to life in a horror film.

His eyes are enormous, his face red, and I can see he's about to yell.

"You don't deserve to be alive! You're worthless!" he screams. "You should have killed yourself when I told you to the first few times. You should still do it now. The world would be much better off without you in it. Do everyone a favor. End it now."

I hear shuffling in the background and I put a hand out to gesture for them to stop. I know they're all there, behind me, ready to destroy this psychopathic loser for saying the stuff he used to on the daily. But we need to let this play out rather than let him out of this the easy way, as tempting as it may be.

I review the cue cards in my hands and as I read, I can't help but flick forward a few. Holy shit, mind blown. So much thought has gone into this game show and I'm here for it. I'm fully on board with what's planned. But I try not to give Brett Wolf any idea about what's happening next. I want him to dream up wild scenarios in his head that won't actually be nearly as bad as what's about to happen to him. As he always taught me, anticipation of the unknown is half the mental torture.

Turning to Brett Wolf, I slow clap. "Wow, Brett Wolf. You must've been waiting a long time to get out all that controlling psycho rage. It must have been building up inside you the entire time you were rotting in prison. In fact, I'm very impressed by all the things you had to say today. So impressed, in fact, that you've earned yourself another bonus prize. Didn't he, guys?"

The four of them step out of the shadows, and each is holding a baseball bat. Slade slaps his bat against the palm of his outstretched hand, creating an ominous smacking sound that echoes off the walls.

"Congratulations! Here is your prize, Brett Wolf! See, these four guys think the opposite of all the things you said, and they have a problem with you lying about me. They protect me. I'm their queen. And I told them what you did to me. They're not very pleased about it. Are you guys?"

I look over at the guys, and they all shake their heads enthusiastically.

"The rule for this bonus prize is one crack each with a baseball bat," I explain to Brett Wolf. "No hitting in the head, because we want to be able to finish out the game. But anywhere else is up for grabs!"

I glance around at each of the guys and their bats, smiling at all four of them, then turn and look at Brett Wolf. "Oh, this is going to be so much fun! I can't wait to see where they pick on your body to make contact with!"

Slade goes first. He stretches the bat high above his head and bends side to side, before twirling the baseball bat over his shoulder and taking a few practice swings.

"First up is Slade!" I call into the microphone. "Slade weighs in at… who the fuck cares, but he's a large guy! His interests include cooking—remember that for later," I chuckle. "He also likes to hide his feelings and pretend he doesn't have any, when really he's constantly simmering just under the surface, ready to boil over at any moment!"

Slade lifts the bat over his left shoulder and brings it down in the center of Brett Wolf's back. It makes a loud cracking sound and sends the man flying by his wrists, his legs lifting in the air. He cries out and swings back and forth by his wrists, scrambling with his toes to find equilibrium.

"Great job, Slade! Come on down, Roman and Aidan! Next up, we have a double whammy! Roman, the house's resident playboy, who is the reason that I am here! Roman prides himself on his good looks and his ability to kill in cold blood, as long as it's profitable. Aidan is a born leader, always thinking five steps ahead, including the most impactful way to inflict pain and injury with one swing of a bat. With Aidan involved, you know this has been well thought through!"

Roman and Aidan stand on either side of Brett Wolf and look at each other, one a lefty, one a righty, and count down, "Three! Two! One! Go!" They nod and raise their bats behind them, and then at the same time, they swing at Brett Wolf, each connecting with a kneecap. He screams as his body flies up behind him, and again he scrambles to find equilibrium.

Brick moves in last. "And last but not least, and probably the one you should be most scared of. It's your new favorite, Brick! You're on his home turf here, in his very own torture basement. It doesn't normally look like this, but he's so excited to entertain you that he had the interior especially designed just for today, and especially for you! Come on down, Brick!"

Brick steps up behind Brett Wolf, who whimpers at the sight of him with the bat in his powerful hands. Brick's eyes are even more wild than usual.

"What are you gonna do?" I ask. "Give him a preview!"

"You never said anything about his balls," says Brick.

He swings his bat up behind him, and Brett Wolf whimpers as he smashes it in front of him, right into Brett Wolf's crotch. The psychopath shrieks in agony as the bat makes contact with a satisfying crack, his legs bending up in the air against his body for a moment before falling back down again. He squeezes his legs together, unsuccessfully trying to find a position where he's not in extreme pain.

"What a fun bonus game! Good job earning that by... how did you earn it again, Brett Wolf?"

"Lying!" He answers without a pause. Clearly he's learning how this game works!

"So you have one more chance, one more life left or you'll lose the game. So speak wisely now. What kind of photography do you like? Let me make it easier for you. We'll do multiple choice. Was it A) pictures of food, B) pictures of your cock, C) inappropriate pictures of humans who it's illegal to have them of?"

"B!" he shrieks.

"And?"

"And C!" he yells without hesitation.

"That's fucking disgusting," I boom into the microphone, starting to get the hang of this hosting gig. "And we just got your confession on tape. Not that you'll have a chance to go anywhere near a courthouse the way you're going. Your freedom is shriveling by the minute. That said, you did technically complete the task, so you're onto the next stage. And... would you believe it? We've got you a special guest to take part in this round! Bring him out, and I'll hand over the microphone to you again, Brick!"

"Slut!" Brett Wolf growls. Even as he bleeds and lays there with grievous bodily harm, he has to get in another sexist insult, trying to get his power back.

"I'm getting really sick of all he has to say right now," growls Slade.

Brick holds up the scalpel he used earlier. I glance at the cold metal tool while I think about the situation.

"I'd like to do it," I say, "but make it the serrated one. I want him to feel this." He grins and nods like it's the proudest I ever made him, and hands the serrated scalpel to me. I strut right up to Brett Wolf with a confidence he's never seen before.

Slade walks over, prying the man's mouth open so I can access his tongue. I extend it as far as I can from his mouth, and then I saw through its fibers, letting the little serrated edges drag across so that they pull on the muscle tissue, like slicing a steak that you need to saw back and forth a little just to get through. He tries to pull his tongue back but Slade helps to keep it sticking out enough for me to cut. Brett Wolf shrieks, hyperventilating, as I finally get to the other side of his tongue, severing it completely. He retches as I hold it up to him, blood pooling in his mouth.

"What's the matter, Brett Wolf?" I ask, batting my eyelashes at him. "Cat... no, what was it? Slut got your tongue?" I grin, and hear Brick cracking up in the background. Roman steps forward and hands me a rag that I use to wipe Brett Wolf's blood and spit off my hands.

Aidan walks over with a plate. He bows and hands it to me. "Ma'am, for later, correct?"

"Yes, we'll need that for later," I reply, unable to prevent my mouth from forming into a small smile as I think about the depravity that 'later' entails.

Slade wheels out an indoor portable stove and a cart with some ingredients all set up to cook. He wears a chef's hat and a fake mustache that makes him look like a hot version of one of the Super Mario Brothers. He places his cart in position in front of Brett Wolf so he'll have a prime position for the cooking session. Chef's counter, if you will.

"Excellent, thank you Angel! Isn't she wonderful?" He winks at me and waves as I leave the main game show 'set' and head back to the shadows to observe what happens next. "Now, Brett Wolf, meet your special guest!"

He looks over as Aidan wheels a man into the room on a dolly cart. He's also tied up and gagged, his eyes frantically trying to acclimate to the wild cacophony of lights and darkness of the basement.

"Here's your cousin Freddy!" booms Brick. "Now, you're already well-acquainted, aren't you? I'll spare the introductions! But don't speak to each other, or Brett Wolf here will receive another bonus prize. And as you know, they get bigger and better every time!"

Both of the men's eyes are like saucers, Freddy grunting but unable to get words through the fabric tied to his face, Brett Wolf too scared to talk. Brett Wolf stares intently at Freddy and zips his lips together as if to reinforce the importance of Freddy not trying to earn him another bonus prize.

"Alright, now we're onto round two. I understand that you and Freddy both sexually assaulted Angel and other women. Is that correct, Brett Wolf?"

I don't know where they found Freddy, but now that I get a good look at him, I remember his face. He was definitely one of the guys Brett Wolf would invite around. Being able to block things out isn't the healthiest defense mechanism, but I'm immensely grateful at times like this when I can't remember all the painful details.

Freddy goes to shake his head, but Brett Wolf is nodding vociferously. He really is a quick learner. I'd say I'm proud of him, but I'm not. He makes my stomach want to hurl out its contents, but it's also quite enjoyable making him squirm.

"This round of the game show is called *Eat a Dick*! We heard you were quite interested in the taste of human flesh, Brett Wolf. So we thought we'd get Freddy to help you out. Keeping it all in the family, some might say!"

Brick hands me the microphone and grabs a very sharp chef's knife from the tool table. He strolls over to Freddy as if he's on a Sunday walk, yanks the man's pants down, pulls his flaccid dick out of his underpants and lops it off with one slice. There's no fanfare this time, just straight-up castration. This man is the means to an end, and we have a lot more planned for the primary focus of this very special event. Freddy screams in agony and writhes in his wrist fastenings, but there's no way he can get free. Blood drips beneath him from the area formally home to his penis.

Brick throws the penis over to Slade, who catches it. He takes a closer look and cringes.

"Glad I'm wearing gloves! And damn, this is an especially ugly one," he laughs.

He clicks the stove on and it lights up with flames on two of the elements. He puts a sauté pan on each and adds a little olive oil and butter to both. "Gives it more flavor. Seasoning is key," he explains to Brett Wolf, winking and nodding at him as if he's his prize pupil in a beginner cooking session. Brett Wolf looks on in horror, coughing and spluttering blood from his de-tongued mouth, the pallor of his skin white as a sheet.

While the oil and butter get hot, he seasons both the penis and the tongue, doing the Salt Bae arm when he adds the salt, causing all of us except for Freddy and Brett Wolf to laugh.

The temperature is where Slade wants it to be, so he puts the penis in one pan and the tongue in the other and they sizzle. The smell isn't great, and I scrunch up my nose, but the reward of seeing him tortured this way is well worth it. I can't wait to see him ace this challenge!

Slade whistles as he skillfully flicks the sauté pans, one in each hand. Once they're done to his liking, he turns off the elements and places the cooked meats on a board to rest. "I find keeping things simple is better in these situations," he explains.

Once they're rested, he places them on a chopping board and slices both along the bias. "It makes it juicier when you cut it this way," he explains, nodding at Brett Wolf. He artfully places them on a plate with a micro green garnish. "To add a little pop of color," he says, gesturing to the dish. "And now we're all set. It's time for you to feast!"

As Brick and Slade approach Brett Wolf with a beautifully plated meal of his cousin's penis and his own tongue, he screams. His body violently flails about and as he gasps to control his breath, he seems like he might be about to pass out. His eyes dart around the room, failing to connect with a particular point. He's feral, out of control, but under our control.

Slade seems in charge of propping Brett Wolf's jaw open tonight, and this time Brick cackles with glee as he feeds spoonfuls of his cousin's dick and his own tongue into his mouth. He gags and tries to spit it out as Brick shovels it in, but Slade clamps his jaw together and growls, "Chew or it's time for another bonus game!" As Brett Wolf whimpers, I see his Adam's apple bobbing wildly as he swallows.

I half-snort, half-gag at what's happening before my eyes.

"Congratulations!" exclaims Brick. "You have passed the *Eat a Dick* challenge! No other contestant has ever got this far!" He beams at Brett Wolf as if he's truly in admiration of his getting to the next point in the game. "To be fair, you're our very first contestant on this game show," he adds. "Ooh, I have an idea! Let's celebrate with a bonus prize." I cackle at the unfairness of it all, Brick's rules changing by the minute. He skips around, clapping his free hand to the microphone and presses an absurd big red button in the center of the room that I didn't notice before. A loud siren goes off, the room lighting up in red and white, on and off, on and off.

Tears pour from Brett Wolf's eyes, his head down and his mouth frozen in a grimace. He makes a whimpering, choking sound. He's not so powerful anymore, now that he can't use his tongue to tear me to shreds.

Brick assesses him, his thumb and forefinger pressed to his chin, and then goes back to the big red button and presses it again.

"Ha! Change of plans, folks. I don't think he could endure what we had planned for this bonus round as well as the finale. And the finale is definitely the most important part of this exercise."

Brett Wolf whimpers again, and this time I sense a twinge of resignation, an understanding that he has no say in what happens next and an understanding that it will not be good for him.

"Alright, Brett Wolf! We picked this final challenge out specifically for you. You should be honored at the attention to detail that went into preparing this. We wouldn't give this challenge to anybody else. It's especially for you, VIP, just like you've always told people you are when you were abusing them. So we've made sure this challenge reflects your power! It's called *See How You Like It!*"

He whimpers and tries to swallow, but it comes out like a splutter. He's going to have to get used to that stump. Or actually, there's probably no point. He won't be around much longer.

Slade walks to the side and collects a sharpie and a piece of paper with a diagram on it.

"Do you know what Slade is holding in his hand, Brett Wolf?"

His eyes are now vacant, the wildness beaten out of him already. He instinctively tries to say 'no', but it turns out you generally need your tongue to say that word, so instead, his mouth just forms a pathetic 'o' shape, a monotone grunt coming out instead. To double down, he shakes his head.

"Slade has a Sharpie in one hand. In the other, he holds a diagram of each and every scar and mark you left on Angel's body. There are 128 of them in total, and there would have been more if you'd had an opportunity to inflict more injuries on her. We are going to draw each and every one on you in exactly the same place as Angel has hers. So we will be here for a while, but once it's done, you will have matching wounds. Isn't it only fitting that you get to experience your own creation for yourself? You're a fucking monster. And you've messed with our Angel. That was a big mistake."

One by one, one-hundred-and-twenty-eight times, Slade asks me which tool or method Brett Wolf used to carve or chisel each of my scars onto my body. With every lash, every slice of metal, every tear of barbed wire, every hot branding iron, scissors, peeler, grater... more blood runs from Brett Wolf. I watch as Brick painstakingly administers each one. After he makes each incision, he goes back to look at the diagram and then compares his handiwork like a proud artist. The entire exercise takes several hours, but it goes by in a flash for me. It's surreal seeing the injuries inflicted on me being inflicted on someone else, to the person who did them to me.

By the time Brick and Slade are done, Brett Wolf has passed out many times and been slapped back to consciousness, so he is forced to endure every sliver of pain.

Freddy, still restrained and dickless, is also passed out, probably from a combination of blood loss, the horror of having his penis chopped off, and what he just saw happen to his cousin.

Brett Wolf's posture sags against his wrist restraints, and like the rest of him, his wrists are bloody and raw. He is flayed, carved, stabbed, hooked, sliced, and butchered, just like me. It's the only thing we ever had in common, and now it's visible. I'd say we are both human, but he's not really human. So that just leaves this. My scars are because of him. And his wounds are because of him as well. The difference is that my conscience is clear.

His eyes are vacant and watery, and he's barely coherent. He slips into semi-consciousness once again. I know he's close to death. But he can't end just drift away quietly, because that would give him control over his final act. This has to end on my terms.

"Brick," I say, my voice firm and calm. "I would like to complete the game now."

Brick nods and hands me the machete. "As you wish, my Valkyrie."

I walk up to Brett Wolf and slap him twice, hard, so that he wakes from his subconscious stupor.

He blinks at me, his vision clearing enough so that recognition dawns in his eyes, snapping him back to where he is. I see pain flash in his gaze as his physical condition registers. All he can see below him is his own blood. And some pieces of dick and tongue meat that fell out of his mouth. His eyes grow wider and he gags.

"Brett Wolf, I'm really sorry, but you didn't pass that last test. What a fucking pussy. I didn't pass out once when you tortured me. Given, you didn't inflict every one of my injuries at one time, but you're still a weak man." I don't love being derogatory about a person's masculinity or lack thereof, but I know it will get to him, so I'm making an exception in the circumstances.

I carefully trim one of my fingernails with the machete and admire the results before turning back to face Brett Wolf.

"And now the time has come for my revenge. You thought you'd turned the tables, that you were going to end my life. But, the truth is, I'm smarter than you and I'm more powerful than you. Always have been, but I just didn't know it. You stripped away my innocence and my youth. You introduced me to evil. You encouraged me to find my darkness. Well, here it is, fucker."

His eyes, despite their fatigue and pain, flash with fear as I let out a guttural scream that echoes off the walls. I lift the machete high above my head and then spin around with it horizontal to the floor. As I pirouette in Brett Wolf's direction, it makes contact with his neck and slices through like butter, just like Brick promised it would.

Brett Wolf's skull bounces to the ground and rolls off to the side.

His body, now separated from his head, crumples to the ground with his wrists still dangling from the shackles.

I walk over and take a closer look at his skull. I need to nudge it with the point of my shoe because it landed face down. His face is like a horror film, his eyes wide and his lips curled in a fearful snarl. Looking down at him, I see how truly pathetic he's always been. He's dead, and he can't hurt me anymore.

It took me a long time to see it, to see that his power was just a construct. He was always as human and vulnerable as anybody else. He was just a complete sicko. Delusional, deranged, a master manipulator. And now he's gone for good.

Brick walks over and does cousin Freddy a favor by injecting him with a lethal concoction of goodness knows what, giving him a more peaceful passage to hell than his cousin.

With the two men who don't belong here dead, the remaining guys all turn to me. Their eyes convey a mixture of emotions—concern, pride, their own fatigue after this extended performance.

Part of me feels numb, but as I take one more peek at his scowling skull something snaps inside me. My body heaves and I gasp for breath as tears burst from my eyes. I'm not much of a crier normally, but my body racks and shudders at the release of having the burden of my psycho removed from me. For hours and hours we tortured this man, and it didn't scratch the surface of the cumulative time he spent inflicting countless horrors on me. Our physical wounds may have matched by the time he died, but he didn't endure the same level of psychological pain that he built up for me prior to and during his crimes. My soul feels crushed, my body heaving at the loss of someone who cared about me more than anyone else in the world, even though that care came in the form of a deadly obsession.

The guys are all looking at me. They're probably wondering if this is what a psychotic break looks like. Maybe that's what's happening to me. I can't stop crying, even though my eyes are swollen and my face is puffy and I'm gasping for breath. He's finally dead, unable to torment me any longer, but it's like a part of me died, too. I'm so glad it's over because this has all been too much. I can't stand any more torture today, no more death. My brain needs to process what just happened, because I feel raw and numb, happy and terrified, energized and exhausted.

As my body wretches and tears continue to cascade from my eyes, Roman steps toward me and wraps an arm around me, pulling my face into his chest, where I continue to sob. His touch is comforting, and finally, I regain my breath with my face buried in his shirt. He continues to hold me, not rushing me, and eventually I look up at him.

"Angel, we're going to clean up here, and get this taken care of," says Aidan, his voice gentle but very much in control, "and then we're going to come and check on you. You don't need to be here for this. Roman will take you upstairs and be with you, okay?"

I nod. Everything seems surreal. Brett Wolf is dead. I always thought he'd kill me. It might take a moment for me to process this.

Roman escorts me upstairs.

"What do you need, Angel? Right now, what do you need most?"

I think about it. "I need a shower," I decide. I can't think of a better thought than washing off the mental and physical residue of Brett Wolf.

"Same," says Roman.

We walk upstairs and Roman leaves me at my door, ready to walk down the hallway to his room.

"Wait." I reach out and grab his hand. He stops, turns and raises an eyebrow. "Stay with me. We can shower together."

"Are you sure?" He arches an eyebrow. "I thought you might want some time to yourself."

"I've never been more sure of anything in my life." I pull him through the bedroom and into the bathroom with me, and shut the door.

I turn the shower on as hot as it will go, and the room fills with steam as we both remove our clothing. I breathe it in deeply, letting the steamy air fill my lungs. Turning the temperature down just a bit, I hop into the shower and pull Roman in with me.

My face paint pours off me and swirls down the drain in a black spiral as Roman and I crowd together under the shower head, our now-wet bodies mashed together. I feel heat generating in my core as my breasts press against his muscular torso. He uses a finger to tilt my head up, and meets my lips in a deep kiss, the warm water splashing down on us. I kiss him back, my tongue pressing against his, hungry for him.

I moan as he dips his head and sucks one of my nipples into his mouth, and rolls the other between his thumb and forefinger. I run my fingers through his dark hair while the water splashes over me, hot and wet, as he teases me.

He stands up and I kiss him again, my arms wrapped tight around his neck.

I reach down and he groans into my mouth as I stroke his hard cock, running my wet hands along his smooth shaft. Fuck, I want him inside me so badly.

He slips his fingers through my folds and slides a single finger inside me, followed by a second. "You're so wet, baby," he rasps. "Did that turn you on back there? Destroying the evil that's haunted you for so long?"

"That, and being naked in a shower with an incredibly hot man who has his fingers in my pussy while I stroke his big, hard cock. That has something to do with it too, I'm pretty sure." I smile up at him and he grins back before kissing me again, this time his tongue exploring mine.

"I want you inside me, Roman," I whisper, my voice husky from the steam and my desire for this incredible man. "Fuck me until I forget everything. Get me dirty while you get me clean. Don't be gentle. I want it rough. I want to feel you for days."

He groans and picks me up, and I wrap my legs tightly around him as he presses my back into the tile behind the shower head, the water continuing to rain down on him as he slides into me in one go. He fucks me hard and fast, and I cry out with every thrust. My clit rubs against his body every time he slams into me.

The combination of the water and steam and the sensations he's generating inside of me create an almost sensory overload, stimulating every part of me. It distracts me from what just happened, my attention focused solely on Roman and the way our bodies meld perfectly together. It almost feels electric, the water creating the sensation of sparks between us.

I scream his name as I come, clenching around his cock while he continues to bury himself deep inside me. His pace increases and he mashes his lips to mine as he comes, releasing into me.

As our orgasms subside, I unwrap my legs from his waist, and he carefully places me on the ground, the water continuing to rain down over us.

"Is that what you had in mind, baby?" he asks, smiling down at me, his arms wrapped protectively around me, the shower continuing to stream warm rivulets between us, on us, around us.

I kiss him again and smile back. "It was absolutely perfect," I whisper. "Thank you for fucking my pain away."

Chapter Nine

Angel

Slade and Brick have me sit between them on the couch. I happily squeeze into the gap, their strong thighs pressing against either side of me.

Each of them laces a hand in mine. They both look at me thoughtfully, as if they're trying to read my every expression, and I lean my head back against the back of the couch so it's easier to glance at both of them.

"How are you feeling?" asks Slade. For once, he's not scowling. He's not smiling, either, but Resting Slade Face is gone for now.

"Okay, I guess. I don't know." I've been asking myself the same question and haven't found the right words to describe it.

"Just okay?" Brick frowns, his disappointment palpable. "I thought today was going to be cathartic for you. That you might feel some excitement, some relief."

I'm not sure how I should frame it for these guys in a way that won't sound ungrateful. It's important that I'm honest and don't pretend that everything is suddenly perfectly okay, but I also want them to know how much I appreciate them making this happen for me. I take a deep breath.

"I'm just processing, I think. I always assumed he would find me and kill me one day. I'm glad that he didn't. I'm glad that we did what we did. That I was able to do what I did. But I don't feel... I don't know how to explain it. I'm glad he's gone. It was exhilarating at the time." I shrug. "There's just a lot to think about."

"Well, you were great," beams Brick. "Gave me a giant boner right in the middle of it, seeing the way you took control down there. I'm so incredibly proud of you... in fact, I'm in awe. And when you sliced off his head, and it rolled around on the floor, I just about came in my pants."

I laugh and Slade snorts. This time, instead of scowling at me, he leans over and kisses me on the cheek. I guess we really are allowed to find the same things funny now.

I feel like I should continue to explain how I'm feeling. They're not pushing me, but saying it aloud is as much about sorting out my own feelings as it's about sharing with them.

"It was vindicating to see him going through some of what he put me through, for sure. And I'm glad he won't be hunting me for the rest of my life, so that brought me closure in a few ways." I sigh, my giddiness wrestling with exhaustion after what has been a monumental day, what may be the hugest of my life. "But no matter what we did to him, no matter how just our revenge was, it still won't bring my family or friends back. It still won't take away my trauma or erase my scars. No matter what you or I ever do, it won't remove my darkness."

"Oh no, baby. Never try to remove your darkness," Brick leans over and kisses me on the forehead. "Your darkness is part of what makes you beautiful. It's electric. It gives you incredible depth and grit and rawness. It's what makes you *you*. Just like your gorgeous scars." He dips his head and kisses a couple of the raised marks on my shoulders. "And it's why you're going to take over the world one day. So channel every sliver of darkness within you, turn it into pure energy, and use it to set the world on fire."

CHAPTER TEN

Angel

The next day

We're all seated around the dining table for breakfast. Normally there's a lot of chit-chat at the table as everyone plans their days, but today things are a little quieter. Somber's not quite the right word because there is an upbeat energy in the air... it's almost as if people are holding back, trying not to be too outwardly cheerful. Maybe everyone is still processing like I am.

Slade cooked for us as usual, but it's not our usual spread. Perhaps unsurprisingly, we're sticking to dry toast with butter and jam. I don't think any of us could stomach anything more after what transpired yesterday. Images of Brett Wolf eating his cousin's penis and his own tongue, and the smell of singed flesh are still etched into my mind, even after I scrubbed myself raw in the shower. I imagine the others feel similarly.

"Hey... so, I know we don't have boundaries, but can we make cannibalism a boundary? Even if we're making somebody else do it?" Aidan asks the table.

Slade gags. "Oh my god, yes can we please? I'm going to follow Brick's lead and go vegan for a while. I'm never going to look at meat the same way again. And seeing I'm the one who cooks around here, you're all coming along for the ride."

"I agree. Human meat is off the menu," says Roman, also gagging as he comments aloud. "Oh my god, I can't believe I'm even saying those words. I'm down for a vegan stint."

Aidan puts a hand across his forehead and shakes his head.

The rest of us half-gag, half-laugh. We're all on the same page about this.

"Okay, unanimous decision. No more of that," says Slade. "Lots of vegetables, grains and seeds on the cards for us until further notice."

Everyone laughs. Including me. Because it's funny and I feel happy.

CHAPTER ELEVEN

Aidan

"I'm glad you're okay." Angel gazes at me, her eyes intense and her brow furrowed. "I feel like an idiot for letting him lure me there. It could have ruined everything. I just couldn't—." My voice trails off.

"What couldn't you?" she asks, placing her hand protectively on my shoulder.

"I couldn't bear the thought of you being taken by him. By him giving you more scars. Of him…" I pause and I can hear my voice wavering even though I try to hold it steady, "of him taking you from us."

Her hand squeezes my shoulder. "You bear so much responsibility. I can see it weighing you down," she says, running her hand down my arm. "It must be exhausting being the voice of reason all the time, when everyone just wants to go out and burn the world down. Feeling like you're responsible for everything."

I exhale deeply. "Yeah, I like that they always want to take action, to protect what's ours," I say, talking about the other guys. "But sometimes the way they go about it isn't in our best interests. I need to reel them back so we think things through. It's okay, I'm used to it now. It's not like it started with them."

"What do you mean?" She looks confused, which is fair. I am being cryptic.

"I'll tell you one day," I say, running a hand through my hair. "Now's not the time. Just know that I'm used to being the one who figures out what needs to happen next."

I don't want to go into it right now. She doesn't need to hear about my sad childhood. About how my parents couldn't care less about my siblings and me. I was second-oldest, but for whatever reason, I became the one who made sure everyone was okay all the time.

I protected them, and I protected myself. Made sure everyone got to the doctor for check-ups and when something was actually wrong, made sure we were all fed and clothed.

Forced my siblings to go to school when my parents couldn't have cared less whether they received an education or stayed holed up in their rooms playing video games or running around shoplifting and getting up to other mischief all day.

They were so wrapped up in their work and their social status, absorbed in their adult lives, full of parties and high society and all that crap, we were just a burden. I think they liked the idea of kids more than actually having them. Being able to say they had four children made them more normal, more palatable, in their social circles. But behind closed doors, there was very little love, very little affection.

My older brother had no idea what the hell was going on, and needed just as much guidance as the younger ones. And so the responsibility to raise my siblings fell to me. I was hardly equipped for the task, but hand on heart, I can say I truly did my best.

When my older brother took his own life while he was still a teenager, it shocked our family, but mainly me. I've always felt like I didn't do enough to guide him, to help him battle his demons and guide him through the dark times. Despite being younger, I very much fell into a parental role with him. But, being older, he had access to drugs and alcohol and sex and lots of people who didn't have his best interests at heart. He used all of those things to escape, to numb the pain. And I can't blame him for an instant.

I'll always wonder if I could have made one tiny change that could have prevented him from doing something so drastic, so final. If I could have noticed more signs, if I would have seen his last panicked text message sooner.

Inevitably, the rest of us grew up, and my remaining siblings came to rely on me less and less. We're still in contact, but I'm once again treated like a sibling, no longer responsible for their personal safety and helping to shape them into functioning adults.

But it's natural for me to assume that role, to take on responsibility for what really should be done by others. It's why I'm so protective of my brotherhood now, I suppose.

"And that's taxing on you," she says, as if she really sees me, as if she truly understands. "There must be so much going on inside your mind that you don't share. Like... deciding to try to rescue me by yourself."

"Ha. Yeah," my mouth tilts up on one side in what I hope is an adorable lopsided smirk. "That didn't work very well, did it, though? One concussion later for me, and those idiots all ended up saving you."

It felt like a repeat of all my past failures, the ones that I bury deep inside me. It was embarrassing, lying there, bound, not being able to free myself or help her. I felt useless, and I was full of fear that Brett Wolf would do something unfixable, irreparable, because

I wasn't there to save her. I didn't care what happened to me, but I was terrified of losing Angel, and I'm still torn up that I didn't get to be the one to save her.

"They're idiots for saving me?" She screws up her nose, and I melt a little at the sight of her adoring smattering of freckles moving on her face.

"Ha, no," I smirk. "They're heroes for saving you. Out of all people, I just thought it would be me who helped to free you, you know? Instead, I lay helpless, bound and gagged with a concussion and a splitting headache, while they rescued you."

"They do need you, you know," she whispers, her fingers trailing gently down the side of my face in front of my ear and down my jaw. Little tingles spread from her touch down my neck. "We all do."

"What did you say?" I ask, my voice husky, another little piece of me melting at her words. I heard her the first time, but I'm desperate to hear it again, her words soothing me in the most perfect way.

"I need you," she says again, tilting her head and pressing her lips to mine.

CHAPTER TWELVE

Brick

Angel pads down the wooden stairs to meet me in the basement. She looks around, and I can tell she's surprised by how quickly the room has returned to its normal state. No more garish carnival of terrors and accompanying cacophony. We're back to the clinical grey business you'd typically expect in a torture basement.

"Wow, you cleaned this quickly. I can't believe the transformation. You guys are amazing."

I shrug. "That entire setting was intended to be for a moment, for a very specific purpose. That moment has passed, and so we're back to business as usual. Everything in its place down here, you know."

She nods, chewing on her lower lip as she glances around. "Anything worth waiting for has a risk of being only temporary," she nods, as if convincing herself of something that seems to be weighing on her mind.

"I saw you looking at the rose on your hand a lot while everything was happening," I say, needing to bring it up. "At the corsage I gave you, I mean." I smile at her, and as the words leave my mouth, I'm sure it sounds like we're at junior prom and I'm seeking approval for my gift.

She laughs, a warm tinkle that echoes gently off the walls. "I've never had a corsage before. It's... cute." She wiggles her wrist to show it off. She went upstairs for a shower and she's put it back on afterwards. "I know it won't last forever and I want to make the most of it. It feels special, having an ornate arrangement adorning my wrist, like it gave me strength in battle or something."

"Cute? Do you really think that?" Cute isn't the word I wanted her to associate it with, although I like she mentions it giving her strength. "You don't really like it, do you?"

"No, I love it!" She explains. "I was actually thinking it would make a really cool tattoo."

I feel my eyes light up. "For real? You know I can do a mean tattoo. I have all the equipment."

"Really? Where?" She looks around the basement and sees that, as usual, everything is immaculately organized. There's definitely no tattoo equipment visible. I make sure I only bring it out when I'm using it. I can't stand unnecessary clutter.

"I keep it in one of the storage cupboards," I explain. "It's been a while since I last did one. I might be a bit rusty."

"I keep learning things about you, Brick. You're quite the enigma." She smiles at me. I love being thought of as an enigma.

"Yeah, I was thinking about going full-time with tattoos before I got into the torture and enforcement business. And then, you know, priorities." I shrug and gesture around the basement. "But I still have all the stuff! I'd love to tattoo you." I'm giddy with excitement at using my needles on her.

"Really? You'd do that for me?" She sounds excited, too, her eyes lighting up, her upper body getting fidgety at the prospect.

"Yeah, definitely," I nod. "If that tattoo would make you happy, of course I'd do it. And I think it's a good idea."

"Why's that? Because it will remind me of you?"

She totally gets me. "Well, that's a great reason. But I'm just so blown away by how you took control of things today. You barely needed us to take down Brett Wolf. You were the lead singer, and we were the backup dancers over there in the corner, just in case."

She laughs. "I still have a mental image of you dancing around in your ridiculous multi-colored sequin jacket with your clown makeup."

I grin. It was a departure from my usual 'uniform', but I know it was just perfect for the occasion.

"I did need to phone a friend when he literally had me backed up in the corner at the place he lured me to," she says, looking down, her voice low. "He would have killed me if you guys hadn't shown up."

"Maybe, although I actually think you would have figured a way out of it. You're quite the fighter," I smile at her. "But seriously. Your future tattoo should remind you that you are fierce, that you took your darkness, and you used it to overcome his evil. You are endlessly strong. He tried to break you, just like he used to when you were younger, over and over again. But you've never let him fully break you. You didn't let him even scratch the surface this time. You saw his words for what they were. Empty, cruel comments to get under your skin and make you feel weak, to distract you from your power. You maintained your control, you escaped from your restraints. And we don't even need to go into what you did in the basement, but it was fucking outstanding."

I think of Brett Wolf's skull bouncing along the ground, his eyes wide. I'm just so proud of her. From the look on her face, I'm guessing she's reliving it, too. Her expression is hard to pinpoint. Maybe a bit proud, but also a little haunted.

"I guess it was kind of cool, not that I plan on making a habit of it," she says. "He was truly a special case."

"So, a tattoo to commemorate your courage for the occasion? To being free of him and being able to move on now?"

She nods. "Well, let's make it happen then, Brick," she grins. "I'm game if you are."

I grin back. This is going to be fun.

Chapter Thirteen

Angel

"You were such a bitch before." I narrow my eyes at Devon.

After some back and forth, we agreed to meet at a wine bar that's on somewhat neutral territory, and we've stepped outside for a cigarette.

So far, we haven't hurled insults or cut each other, so we're off to a reasonable start.

I was a little surprised when Devon reached out and said she wanted to meet, but the entire ordeal with Brett Wolf has given me a little perspective, and I'm willing to cut her some slack. She might be a bitch, but she's done nothing to truly hurt me. Rudeness seems too benign to warrant a full-blown feud, and I'm realizing we have a lot more to gain by partnering together.

Devon and I are standing in a back alleyway that runs along the side of the back entrance to the wine bar. We both lean against the brick wall, which is painted a very pale lemon cream color, our shoes crunching on the loose gravel underfoot. We're shaded by tall palm trees that sway gently in the breeze, and even though we're not directly by the ocean, the air still has a briny note to it.

The sky is a brilliant blue, with fluffy white clouds making pleasantly geometrical rolling shapes as far as the eye can see. Despite all the drama we've been experiencing, this really is a beautiful location.

"So were you. And I still am," she shrugs. "I have a feeling you are too, and that's fine. We just have much bigger fish to fry than being bitchy to each other. Consider this a truce, at least temporarily?"

I glance at her in an attempt to see if she's playing games, if she has some type of ulterior motive. But she seems genuine and I don't really see another option. "Deal."

We nod at each other in silent agreement.

"So I think we're aligned," she says, squinting at me as if trying to confirm we really are on the same page. "They need each other. They have no chance of taking control without leveraging each other's strengths."

"Right," I reply, nodding. "Alone, I don't think either group has the full set of skills needed and we risk losing the people we care about most if we let them continue along the way they've been going."

"I'm concerned they'll never listen to us, though," I sigh. "This is a lot for them, and we might be asking more than they're prepared to give."

I frown, trying to figure out how to approach my guys with our plan. As much as they care about me, I don't know how much they'll appreciate me meddling in their business, especially given how tense things have been between the two groups.

"Hell, I never thought I'd find myself saying this either, you know. But people can change their minds," she shrugs.

"Ditto. But here we are. So maybe you're right." She has a point. People evolve over time, people can change. Although I have a feeling that she and I are more open-minded and less stubborn than any of our guys.

She leans back against the wall, one foot propped up, and takes a drag from her cigarette, surveying me. She lets out a long exhale, plumes of smoke billowing from her mouth and nostrils. "You look worried still."

"I'm just still not sure how to convince them of this. All they do is complain about your guys." Some days I think if I hear about the 'snake guys' one more time, I'm going to scream. My men are always talking about what small fries they are, but they seem to take up a heck of a lot of real estate in each of their heads.

"Same, I'm super sick of hearing all about 'the Brixtons this, the Brixtons that'. But I'm sure you'll find a way. We both will. There's no doubt in my mind you can be quite persuasive." She smirks at me. "Clearly, they care about you. Just use what you have. Make sure there's something in it for you, too. That's what I do."

I peer at her. "You mean...?"

She smirks at me again and takes another drag on her cigarette and then stubs it out on the ground before turning and gesturing for us to head back inside. "You'll figure it out."

We return to the wine bar, where we sit back down at the bar-top and raise our champagne flutes. "Here's hoping we get this figured out and soon," I toast. "It's the only way we'll all get what we want."

"To getting what we want," she replies.

We clink our glasses together, solidifying our truce and our plan.

The guys would be pissed if they knew we were meeting like this. That we were forging a bond between rivals and planning for them to build an alliance. It's the last thing any of them would be in favor of.

But we can see that it truly might be the only way we can get them what they want.

What we all want.

Control of the islands, and to get rid of Tane Brown for good.

Chapter Fourteen

Brick

Angel watches me closely as I set up my tattoo equipment. I enjoy the attention of her gaze. It makes me feel a little giddy, giving me an opportunity to show off to her. These days, the thing that matters most to me is Angel's approval.

I bring out my custom-made tattoo bed, black leather with a Swarovski skull pattern weaving its way across the dark surface. It's one of my great pride and joys, other than my torture basement, of course.

And now Angel is rapidly approaching number one on that list. She's quickly becoming my pride and joy, too. And now I get to permanently decorate her gorgeous body.

"That's a nice chair," she says, circling it and taking in all its features. She runs a hand gently across the headrest, feeling the fabric against her fingers. "Is that real leather? It's so soft."

"Yep, I designed it myself," I grin and run my hand over it as well, enjoying the cool sensation. "Brought it over from the mainland when we moved. I couldn't let her go, she's my baby. Extendable headrest, hydraulic base, touch-sensor remote. Took me ages to find just the right specs."

"Talk dirty to me," she wiggles her eyebrows. "I've been wanting something like this for the salon for so long."

"Oh yeah? Like you want a combined hair salon and tattoo parlor?"

"Why not? A one-stop shop for making people feel their best, and bringing out the best in them."

"I love it," I grin. I love how we're always on the same page. She's creative, I'm creative. I mean, her creativity is usually about making people look and feel their best, and mine is about making them look and feel their worst... but we just get each other. Kindred spirits.

I place a sketchpad and pencils on the desk in front of me, alongside my tattoo guns, ink, needles and towels, along with a box of disposable gloves. I'm just as methodical when it comes to my tattoo work as I am when it comes to torture.

The difference with the tattooing is that I actually get to see my artwork live on with its human canvases, unlike my torture victims. I get a thrill from seeing their body art out in their day-to-day life, knowing I marked them up that way. So I like to make sure they heal properly so they look their best, and I have all the necessary bandages and ointment at the ready as well.

I'm so excited to tattoo Angel. I'm thrilled she liked the corsage I got her so much that she wants a permanent reminder of it. But more than that, I'm thrilled that she understood the meaning behind it, what drove me to get it for her on that day of all days. Because I meant every word I said.

I take hold of her hand, and anchor it still against the armrest as I sketch out the tattoo.

She jumps at the sensation of the cool pen on the back of her hand. "Are you ticklish, Angel?"

She laughs. "Maybe just a little. And the pen is cold and wet."

I grin back at her. "Hold still, or you'll end up with something you don't want."

I listen as she chats away about tattoos she's had done in the past. She tells a funny story about a friend who really did end up with a tattoo they didn't ask for after an awkward miscommunication with an artist.

"I promise that won't happen to you, Angel," I say, smiling at her.

"I know," she smiles at me through her long, thick eyelashes. "I trust you."

My heart melts a little. I can tell she means it, that she truly trusts me. And she knows what I'm capable of. Most people are terrified of me, whether just based on the way I look or actually because they know what I do for work. How I delight in cracking human bones and inflicting worlds of pain on people by the dozen. But not Angel. Here she sits, vulnerable and trusting of me. It's a rare feeling, and it makes me feel warm inside, which I'm not used to.

After a while of deep concentration, I complete the sketch on the back of her hand.

"What do you think?" I hold her by the wrist and tip her hand up so she can see the full design.

She tilts her hand back and forth so she can see all the angles. "Oh wow, Brick," she gasps, assessing every inch of the design. "You really are talented. I wouldn't change a thing. You've really thought about how this would look like as my hand moves, and it's just perfect. I can't wait to see what it looks like when it's done."

Angel always knows the right things to say to make a guy feel great.

The tattoo gun buzzes as I outline the rose on the back of her hand. As I glide the gun over the bonier parts of her hand, she grits her teeth, and a couple of times I hear a sharp intake of breath. But mostly, she just tilts her head back, closing her eyes and arching her back. I can tell she's enjoying the feel of the needle buzzing against her skin, finding pleasure in the pain.

I concentrate, biting my lower lip as I trace fine lines and add shading and other details. This tattoo has to be perfect, just like Angel. She deserves nothing but the best. She's going to take it with her everywhere she goes, and it needs to be as beautiful as she is inside and out. As the needle buzzes over her hand, where most people flinch, she watches with interest and a slight flush develops on face.

"You're enjoying the feeling, aren't you?" I ask her.

"Yeah," she bites her lower lip as she nods at me. "That's partly why I have so many tattoos," she says. "I enjoy the way they feel."

The entire process takes around three hours, but she never complains, just watches with interest, and frankly with what seems to be arousal. Which gets me going as well.

I've tattooed people who have shrieked and just about passed out, and sworn, and even hit me as I've worked on them. Everyone's response is unique. I've heard the same from friends of mine who do it professionally. But Angel is a true pro, taking it like a champ. Savoring it.

Once the tattoo is finally complete, I let her take a look. She tilts her hand back and forth again to see all the angles of the finished work. She gasps. "Oh, it's even more beautiful than I thought it would be. Thank you, Brick!"

She smiles at me and my heart melts a little more. Okay, and my dick gets a little hard as well.

I smile back at her as I gently cover it with a tattoo bandage. "Keep this on for at least two days, then you can remove it and start putting on this ointment a few times a day for a couple of weeks, just so it doesn't dry out."

"Yes, Doctor Brick," she grins at me. "You know I have hd tattoos before, right? I know the drill."

"Yeah, but I don't know what those lunatic artists you've been working with have advised you, do I?" I shrug. "There's so much conflicting aftercare information out there. I want to make sure you have the best advice directly from me." I smile at her.

"You're definitely the biggest lunatic that I've ever let tattoo me." She grins at me again through her lashes, raising her non-tattooed hand and running her fingers gently along my jaw. Jesus. The things this woman does to me just by being herself all the fucking time. The way she makes me feel so amazing. It's the little things, sometimes, that mean the most.

"So you really like the pain of being tattooed, huh?" I really am impressed by the way she handled the pain, and turned on by how much she seemed to enjoy it.

"Mmm yeah," she says, gesturing at her body, which is covered in them. "I guess you could say that."

"I know another place with more nerve endings." I bite my lower lip, trailing my eyes to her gorgeous mouth, down to her core, and then back up to meet her gaze.

"Oh yeah," she whispers. "Why don't you show me?"

My cock is rock hard at the thought of all of her nerve centers and what I want to do with them.

She locks eyes with me as I reach out three of my fingers and rub her pussy through her shorts. She arches her back some more and moans, grinding herself against my hand.

"Would you like me to continue?" I ask, continuing to rub her. "I think it would be better if you were wearing less clothing, though. Maybe none at all."

She nods at me, biting her lower lip. "Mmhmm," she moans.

I pull down her shorts and she lifts her hips so I can get them over her ass, and I slide them down her legs and toss them to the side. The scent of her arousal immediately fills the room. God, she's fucking fantastic.

"Your panties are soaking, Angel," I growl. "Being tattooed really does turn you on."

She gives me a sexy grin, her eyes half-lidded. "It helps when your tattoo artist is hot as fuck."

I involuntarily beam as I slide her panties off and throw them onto the ground near her shorts.

I yank her knees apart, spreading her thighs to reveal her slick folds, and run a finger up her slit. I pull it away, coated in her arousal, and press it to her lips. She takes my finger in her hand and pulls it to her mouth, licking off every drop of her juices. I groan as her tongue circles my finger, wrestling with it.

I return my hand between her legs and rub at her clit. She moans as I trace the distance from her entrance and back to her clit, and then massage it with more pressure and more speed. "Oh fuck, Brick!"

"Can I tattoo you somewhere more sensitive?" I ask, not wanting the tattoo session to end. I'm feeling spontaneous, and I hope she is, too. The things I want to do to her, this divine Valkyrie of mine.

"Yes," she gasps, as I continue to manipulate her clit with my fingers. She bucks her hips at me, and I increase the pace of my touch.

"Can I really tattoo you more, baby?" I hope she's not just teasing. I have plans for her if she's open to it.

"Yes," she gasps, rolling her hips and arching them toward my fingers. "You can."

"Do you trust me to do anything I want?" I slide two fingers inside her while continuing to manipulate her clit with my thumb, and she moans and bucks her hips even more wildly.

"I'm going to have to stop playing with your pussy for a moment," I say, "or your tattoo's going to be a series of squiggly lines, the way you're bucking your soaking cunt around all over my fingers."

She pouts as I pull my fingers out of her.

"Promise you won't stop for too long," she pants. "That felt too good to be the end of it."

"Oh, I promise, Angel," I smile at her. "I'll take good care of you and make sure you get exactly what you need."

She smiles back at me in anticipation.

I set up the gun again, this time with hot pink ink. This is going to be something small between us, to mark the occasion and to remind her of me.

I use my non-tattooing hand to pull her leg up and to the right, keeping her bare pussy exposed to me. She hisses as I tattoo a small pink heart on her inner thigh, and more arousal trickles out of her entrance.

Jesus. I need to be inside her as soon as possible. My cock is rock hard and ready to go, and I can see that she is, too. I place the tattoo gun carefully on the table beside the tattooing chair.

"You're a dirty girl, aren't you, Angel? Getting off on this pain. I can see how it turns you on and makes your cunt beg to be stuffed."

I slide two fingers inside her again, and she moans and grinds against the flat of my hand with her clit.

Using my now-free hand, I wipe off the tattoo with a cloth. "There you go. Now you'll always remember me. I've marked you with something special, something intimate, just for us."

"What about this, though?" She holds up her hand.

"That's a reminder of how powerful you are. Of what you were able to do that day. Of how you own your darkness." I point to her inner thigh. "Now this, on the other hand," I say, dipping my head to plant a kiss on her freshly tattooed skin. "This is a reminder of me, and how much I love your pussy. Of how you belong to me."

She smiles down at me, and the combination of her gorgeous face signaling approval, as well as the view of her soaking pussy and her new tattoo, are all enough to almost make me come in my pants.

I dip my head down and lap at her arousal, which is quickly becoming a puddle on my custom-made tattoo recliner. At this rate, I'm going to need a replacement, but as much as I love this chair, I'm not mad about it.

She squeezes her legs around my neck as I feast on her, wrapping my arms around her from underneath her thighs to hold her still, so she just has to sit there and take it. My tongue laps at her clit, twirling and flicking. I suck her clit into my mouth right as I slide two fingers inside of her and her hips fly into the air, an orgasm hitting her with force at my touch.

I hold my face to her pussy as she bucks, and I feel arousal coursing out of her, coating my mouth and my chin. I keep my tongue on her clit, lapping and sucking as she writhes against my face, still coming down from her peak, teasing her through her increased sensitivity.

"Fuck me," she begs, panting, trying to pull me up by my shoulders. "Please, I need you to bury your cock deep inside me."

I growl at the thought of slamming myself inside her, right to my hilt. I can't wait to feel her wet walls against my cock.

But first I want her mouth on me. "Suck my cock first, baby," I say, standing up and moving closer to her face. "I want your lips wrapped around me."

She licks her lips as she gazes at my cock. It's roughly at her eye level.

I grab a handful of her hair and pull her face down on it. She opens her mouth and takes it down into her throat, letting me slide it almost all the way in. I hear her saliva swish against my cock, a satisfyingly sloppy attempt at deep throating my shaft.

As I thrust my hips to sink my cock into her mouth over and over again, she grabs my balls in one hand and twirls them around, gently twisting and squeezing. I use my hold on her hair to raise and lower her head so that her mouth bobs up and down on my cock while she expertly sucks and licks at my shaft and tip.

"Fucking hell, Angel," I rasp. "Your mouth feels amazing on my cock. Those lips are insane."

She hums a response, causing vibrations from her mouth to ripple across my shaft and I groan, slamming her face onto my hardness.

"I need your pussy, baby," I growl. "You can do this again later, but I need to be inside you right now."

I pull her head away from my cock and she leans back in the chair. "Get on all fours and stick your ass in the air," I direct her, and she flips over, her creamy ass sticking up high to reveal her soaking pussy and her tiny asshole from behind. I use the hydraulic pump to get her to the perfect level, so her pussy is lined up with my cock. This chair has its advantages beyond convenience while tattooing, like a super advanced sex wedge guaranteeing nothing but perfect angles.

"Your cunt is so fucking wet," I growl as I look at it, in the air and glistening at me, inviting me to plunge myself deep inside her.

I smack her on her ass and her body trembles, a little arousal trickling out of her. I dip my finger into it and she gasps as I smear her juices across her back entrance.

"You like that, baby," I ask. "Does my little angel of death want me to stick my finger in her asshole?"

"Mmmhmm," she moans. "Please, I want to feel you inside both holes at once. Fill me up, daddy."

"That's my dirty fucking angel," I growl as I trace her cream around her puckered entrance. I spank her hard on one of her cheeks and she moans, sticking her ass up further in the air as if she wants me to do it again. "I'm going to fill you up and fuck you until you can't breathe, until you see stars."

She moans and I spank her again.

I work a finger inside her ass. She clenches tightly against me, and I thrust my finger in and out of her. She grinds her hips backward as if she wants my finger deeper inside.

"Please, baby. Harder. Faster. More," she begs.

"Good girl," I bend over her back and growl into her ear. "Begging for more like a dirty slut. Do you want my cock now, while I keep fingering your little asshole?"

"Yes, please. Fuck me," she moans.

"You're going to need to spread your thighs apart, baby. I need extra room. I'm bigger than my brothers," I growl, and she moans in response, obediently spreading her knees wide on the chair until they're almost falling off either side. "Good fucking girl," I groan as I look at her glistening pussy, bared to me and hungrily awaiting my engorged cock.

I line myself up with her entrance and slam my cock into her in one thrust, burying myself in her soaking cunt.

"Fuck!" she screams as I slam into her, driving my cock as deep as it can go, filling her up.

My piercing drags along her walls and she groans. "Oh my fucking god, your piercing. It feels incredible. I want more. Harder!"

I hold her hips steady and I tease her with a few gentle, slow thrusts, pulling myself almost the full way out and then slowly gliding my entire length into her and burying myself to her hilt.

She tries to rock against me but I hold her still, controlling our movements.

I reach a hand around her waist, trailing it downward until I reach her clit and she gasps at my touch, angling her mound into my hand to increase the pressure. I stroke her pussy while I continue to thrust in and out of her.

"Oh fuck, I'm about to come," she moans, using her hips to back further onto my cock. "Brick, you feel so fucking good!"

"Good girl," I groan, my voice husky with desire. "Come for me, baby. Come all over my big hard cock."

Her body tenses, and I feel her pussy clench around my shaft as her hips buck and writhe in front of me. I hold them as still as possible, but she still manages to thrash around wildly on my cock as her orgasm takes over. Finally, it subsides, and she leans forward, panting.

"I want your ass, Angel," I growl, still hard and craving more of her. "Are you ready for that?"

I trail my finger back over her asshole, still slick with the lubrication of her arousal, and she moans softly.

"Fuck me in the ass, Brick," she moans. "I want it hard."

"Are you sure, baby? Because I won't be gentle."

"I'm very sure," she rasps. "Give it to me, baby."

I groan and slide out of her pussy and trail my cock up her taint, finding her back entrance. My cock is coated slick with her juices and I slide in the tip gently at first, but then keep going until I'm buried deep inside her tight little asshole.

"Fuck!" she gasps as I squeeze her by the hips. "That piercing again!" I hold her still once again as I thrust in and out of her.

"You're a good girl, taking my enormous cock deep in your ass after letting me fuck your pussy so hard," I grind out, and she moans in response, her voice husky and sexy as hell.

My thrusts intensify in their pace and intensity, and she cries out as I use my cock to rail her ass. She clenches against me as I reach down and squeeze her clit, and it sends me over the edge. I fill her up, releasing deep inside her ass, and she arches her back, grinding against me and clamping her ass on my cock as if she's trying to milk me of every last drop.

I pull out, and a combination of my cum and her arousal spills from her ass onto the chair. It's an expensive chair, custom-made and irreplaceable. But I don't fucking care. I hope it leaves a stain that will remind me of this moment forever. My angel of death, letting me tattoo her and then burying my cock in all three of her gorgeous holes. I will never ever forget this moment.

I flip her back over and lift up her bandaged hand, kissing it softly.

"Thank you for letting me mark you," I say. "I hope it's done you adequate justice. You're so beautiful, you know. And you deserve only the best."

Her eyes meet mine and she smiles, but I still detect a tinge of sadness in her joy. I know the last few days have been a lot, and while much of it has been positive, she has a myriad of emotions simmering just below the surface. While I'll do my best to distract her and ease her pain, I know it won't just go away overnight.

"Nobody has ever done anything like this for me before, Brick," she whispers, her eyes on the verge of tears as she admires the back of her hand once again. "Thank you."

"Anything for you," I whisper back, and kiss her hand again. I dip my head down and kiss her upper thigh again as well.

And I truly mean it.

I would do anything for this woman.

Anything at all.

Chapter Fifteen

Aidan

"For the fucking last time, leave us alone," I growl. "We have an arrangement. You're not meant to be slowing us down. You're fucking with our profits."

I'm beyond sick of these snake guys compromising our potential to grow as rapidly as possible. It's time to put a stop to it once and for all.

"You compromised the arrangement when you fucked with Devon," Zeke growls back, his eyes narrowing.

"We didn't *fuck with* Devon, *Zeke*." I can't help but spit out his name. He's so condescending, I can't stand him. "Angel was just being inquisitive. She didn't mean to blow up your relationship."

"You could never blow up our relationship," he scoffs. "That's the last thing I'm worried about. What we have is much too strong for the likes of you to have any impact on, no matter how hard you try to mess it up. But I don't believe a fucking word you say, bro. Like there wasn't an agenda letting her know about the debt repayment. Trying to pass it off as an innocent mistake. You're an absolute joke!"

"You're the jokes around here!" Slade snarls. "You won't even do your job properly. Making up stupid rules to get out of the actual work!"

"Because we won't murder people in cold blood or move hard drugs?" Skyler narrows his eyes at Slade. None of us like each other, but those two seem to have a particular dislike for each other. Then again, Slade has a particular dislike for lots of people, including Angel until very recently.

"Yeah, you're weak," sneers Slade. "You'll never be anything like us."

"You're the fucking weak ones. You'll do anything for money, no matter what it costs, if that makes sense. You're so fucking hungry for power you don't care about being human."

"Yeah? That's what you think? It's sure paying off for us. We've eclipsed you in, what… eighteen months?" I'm proud of what we've been able to accomplish in such a short time, and I don't mind rubbing it in. These guys have been so complacent, they've had a home-court advantage for so many years and have squandered it away. What a missed opportunity. I don't know that they're even smart enough to comprehend that, though, let alone regret it. They seem lazy, disorganized, the polar opposite of us.

"Sometimes power doesn't come from money," Skyler furrows his brow, his words coming out in a snarl.

"You're ridiculous," I smirk. "Your father would be ashamed of how you're butchering his legacy, Skyler."

Skyler's eyes darken, and he spits in my direction. "Don't you fucking dish out what you can't take."

I can't handle him spitting on me. In an uncharacteristically reactive and impulsive move, I throw a punch at Skyler and it glances off his jaw. He spins around and tries to upper-cut me but he partially misses. Still, his fist glances off my lip, splitting it and sending blood flying.

This only pisses me off more. I swing at him and connect with his jaw. His face jerks back hard and saliva flies from his mouth, my knuckles stinging at the impact. That was a good one.

He regains composure and punches me back, this time connecting with my jaw and sending my head flying back. My neck twinges as it bobs around in response to the impact like a crash test dummy. It's been a while since I fought like this. My adrenalin is racing, and I can only imagine this is how Brick feels like on the regular.

I see Slade beginning to circle Dom, his fists ready to fight. Skyler regains his fighting posture as well and moves closer to me. This could go on all day at this rate.

"Come on, Slade," I say, suddenly regaining my rationality. "This isn't going anywhere. It's not worth our time."

Slade spits at Dom, and Dom snarls. The glob of saliva barely misses him. And thankfully, it didn't make contact, or I think this entire fight would have just started up all over again.

"Slade! That's enough. Come on, let's go." I wipe my lip with the back of my hand and motion for the others to follow.

"You fucking started the fighting," snarls Slade, glaring at me.

"You're right, I did," I reply, glaring back at him. "And now I'm finishing it."

Chapter Sixteen

Roman

We pull up to a quiet road. A middle-aged man in overalls is walking toward his car, which is curbside a little further up the street. We've studied his routine, and know this is where he parks his car while he's at work. He finishes up this time of day like clockwork.

He doesn't notice as we pull to the side of the road and get out of our vehicle, or as we walk toward him purposefully, our pace faster than his as we gain on him. As he reaches for the handle on the driver's door, Brick taps him on the shoulder. He turns, surprised, and his eyes grow large as he sees two large men towering over him. He pays particular attention to Brick, who, as usual, is looking a little unhinged, his eyes wildly flitting around, taking in his surroundings and then honing in on the man.

"Hello, Billy," growls Brick.

"Who—who the fuck are you, and how do you know my name?" He tries to get into the car, but Brick grabs him by the back of his collar and holds him just out of reach of the car door. He's a fairly big guy, but Brick is enormous and visibly stronger.

"We're your worst nightmare, Billy. Avenging angels, if you will." Brick grins broadly at the man.

"What? Avenging for what? I don't get it." His eyes narrow and he shakes his head slightly. His confusion seems genuine. Maybe he has a lot of things that are worth avenging.

"Have you been to a club called *Temptation*, Billy?" asks Brick, his voice low and his words precise. "Think carefully before you answer, because we don't tolerate lying. We've cut men's tongues out for less. Literally just the other day we did that to someone, didn't we, Roman?"

I nod and shrug. "It's true. Although, to be fair, they did far worse than you did."

"It still could be a good option, though," says Brick, "depending on how you play your cards."

Billy's face grows ashen. "I—yes, I know the club you mean. I've been there once or twice." His gaze travels to the floor.

"That's our club, Billy," I say in a low tone. "We're the owners."

His face falls further. "Oh," he says, his voice low.

"Yeah, 'oh' is right, Billy. Do you really think we're going to tolerate a piece of shit like you coming into our club and roughing up our girls?"

"I don't know what you're talking about," says Billy, jutting his jaw out. His spooked eyes betray his attempt to feign ignorance.

I roll my eyes. "We have you on camera, Billy. It would be stupid of you to deny it when we can literally see you with your dick out."

"It wasn't me," he frowns, almost whiny in his denial. "You must have me mistaken for somebody else."

"Would you like to pull your dick out for comparison purposes? It's probably better if you just confess to what you did, because Brick has a very sharp knife in his pocket and he doesn't enjoy looking at other men's dicks."

Brick pulls the knife out of his pocket and flicks open the blade, grinning at Billy. "I've been wanting to test this out. Sharpened it just this morning."

If Billy could shrink into himself any further, he'd completely disappear. His eyes dart around, looking for an escape that doesn't come.

"The dancer you attacked. Melissa is her name. She identified you as well."

He narrows his eyes. "I don't know a Melissa. Dumb bitch probably made it up. Trying to get money off me or something."

Without hesitating, Brick swings his giant flat-knuckled fist at Billy and a cracking sound rings out as it crunches into the man's broad nose.

Billy groans and grabs at his face. "Jesus! Okay, okay. I might have gotten a little handsy. Meant nothing by it."

"We have a strict rule that anyone who hurts our staff gets a lifetime ban," I explain, shrugging. "And not just from the club. From the island."

He glares at me, blood gushing out of his nose, turning his lips a scarlet red. "Oh yeah? I've lived here my whole life, unlike you mainland fucks. You think you can kick me off my own island?"

"We don't just think we can," I growl. "We know we can."

"Would you like us to come and help you pack, or do you think you can get your own things together and get out of here in the next 24 hours?" Brick asks.

"You won't be able to find me," he says, his voice smug. "I know this island better than you. I have plenty of places to hide if I want to. My network is extensive."

"That's where you're wrong, Billy," I reply, my voice steady. "We know you live with your wife, Janice, over on Monterey Street. We know your children attend the local elementary and middle schools two blocks over."

"Yep," says Brick, nodding in agreement. "We also know you work at the auto parts store and your boss's name is..." Brick clicks his fingers, his eyes flitting up and to the side as he tries to recall the name. "Sam, that's it, Sam. He was very interested to hear that you're going to be visiting the mainland on some family business. He won't be expecting you around for a while. It was so nice of him to grant you an indefinite leave of absence under the circumstances."

"Wha—how?" I didn't think Billy's face could get any paler, but it does. His eyes flatten with defeat, his shoulders slumping in resignation.

"Billy, you underestimate us," I say, shrugging, my eyes locked on his. "We may not have grown up here, but we're like bacteria. Our networks have spread exponentially and we know everything there is to know about sorry little assholes like yourself who have nothing better to do than try to feel up and rape women who are trying to earn an honest day's pay. So unless you'd like Janice to receive photo evidence of you trying to shove your cock inside one of our dancers, and unless you'd like your kids to read about your rapist tendencies and other proclivities in the local papers, we suggest you get yourself to the mainland as soon as possible. Oh, and don't get any wise ideas. We'll be watching and waiting. And if you don't get out of here by this time tomorrow evening? We'll chop you into tiny little pieces and mail you to the mainland as a warning to anybody who wants to fuck with us. Do you understand?"

"Ye—yes," he stammers, nodding fast.

"We will be watching. No funny business, Billy."

"Okay, yes," he nods, his eyes like saucers. "I'll leave right away."

"Great. Now that wasn't so hard, was it Billy?" I smile at him, glad he finally under-stands the severity of the situation.

"No, it wasn't."

Brick says, "One more thing, Billy."

Billy turns to look at him and Brick grabs him by the shoulders. He rears his knee back and rams it forward, right into Billy's nuts. Billy groans as he crumples to the ground. "That was for Melissa."

Chapter Seventeen

Angel

"**I** want to pierce you," Brick growls.

"Oh yeah?" The combination of his husky voice and my imagination cause my pussy to clench. "You just tattooed me... twice, even... and now you want to pierce me, too?"

"Mmhmm." He bites his lower lip and his eyes trail down my body, stopping at my pussy. "Down there."

"Like... my pussy?"

"Yep. Clitoral hood. Vertical."

Slade coughs. "How long does that take to heal, Brick?"

He shrugs. "Something like six to eight weeks."

"We get a say before you do something extreme like that, bro," says Aidan. "If she's going to be out of commission while it heals, especially for that long, we get a say."

"There are other things we can do for that time."

"Hey! It's my body. I get a say as well." I laugh. Fucking idiots talking about putting holes and other things in my body like I'm not even there. I have heard having a piercing like that feels incredible, though. And with the amount of attention that part of my body has been getting lately, why not magnify the pleasure?

"I'd be keen," I say, winking at Brick. "But let's pick the right time. I feel like we have some things to get out of all of our systems before there's any downtime... there."

Four pairs of eyes explore my body with hunger. Fucking hell. Living with four hot men, you'd think I'd have enough, too much even. But every moment I spend with them, every time any of us are intimate, leaves me craving more. They're turning me into an insatiable sex fiend. Which they all seem to be totally fine with. Now that I think about it, so am I.

Brick scoops me up in his arms, one hand around my waist and the other under my knees. I wrap my arms around his neck and laugh. "Sorry, guys. I need to go show her why she needs one. Research," he adds. I giggle as he races out of the room with me and carries me up to his room.

He lays me down on the bed and carefully peels off my pants. He caresses my slit through my panties, and I can feel the material is getting soaked through.

"You're so wet, Angel, thinking about me piercing you. It's got you all hot and bothered, hasn't it, you dirty girl?" He grins down at me.

I smile up at him. "Maybe."

"Good. Would you like to hear about what it will feel like, while I'm doing it and after?"

"Mmhmm," I say, as he continues to stroke my pussy through my panties.

"I'm going to have to demonstrate," he says, sliding my panties off. He spreads my thighs apart so my legs are wide open, exposing my pussy.

He grabs a hand mirror from the dresser and holds it up to me with one hand. I watch as he strokes my slit up to my clit and back down, my pussy clenching as I watch him touch me in the reflection. He inserts a finger in my entrance, and when he removes it I watch some of my arousal trickle out onto the bedsheets.

"So when I pierce your clitoral hood," he points at it and then rubs it a little, "I'm going to do it vertically because that's meant to feel the best for you. That means I'm going to take this piece of skin that protects your gorgeous clit that I enjoy sucking on so much, and I'm going to stick a needle through it." He motions like he's piercing me, and I moan at the thought of him sticking a needle through one of my most intimate areas. "It's going to hurt a lot for just a moment, and I know you'll enjoy the pain. I want to look into your eyes as the needle passes through your flesh. Your clit will throb for a while, and it won't be comfortable. But in a month or two, it will heal completely. And then," he kisses my clit softly, "I'll be able to use my tongue to move the metal around, and it will pull on your clit and drag against it in the best way."

"Like your cock piercing drags along my walls?" I inhale deeply at the thought of the exquisite way his piercing feels when he's inside me.

"Exactly. And I will suck it into my mouth and tug on it until you scream." He sucks my clit into his mouth, simulating what he would do with the piercing. I moan as his teeth tug gently on my clit, causing ripples of pleasure to emanate down into my thighs and up into my belly. If it feels this good without the piercing, I can only imagine the sensations I'll feel when he tugs on that.

"Oh fuck, Brick," I moan as he flicks his tongue across my clit.

I pull my face away, replacing it with a finger and stroking languidly at her swollen nub. "And then do you know what I'll do?"

"No, what?"

He hooks his thumbs into his waistband and slides off his own pants. His cock is rock hard. He leans over me and lines it up with my entrance, and glides it into my wetness in one thrust.

"Then I'm going to get on top of you, just like this. And I'm going to slide my cock into your sweet cunt, making sure I press down on your clit so that your piercing drags against my skin, pulling back and forth, giving you pleasure. Do you want that?"

"Yes, I want that," I moan, arching my hips toward him, granting him deeper access to my pussy.

"I'll grab it with my teeth and tug on it until it hurts, until you beg me to stop because you don't think it can stretch any further." He reaches down and pinches my clit hard and I cry out, a ripple of pleasure and pain radiating down my inner thighs.

"And then," he growls, "you're going to flip over like a good girl and sit on my big, hard cock." He twists his hips so that we roll and he flips me onto him, my pussy still impaled on his iron-like hardness. "And then you're going to ride me and tilt your pelvis so that your piercing rubs against me until you can't bear it anymore."

I rock my hips, grinding against him. It stimulates my clit without the piercing and I moan. I can't even begin to fathom how much extra pleasure the piercing will add.

"So, you want me to do it, don't you, Angel?" he asks, his gaze locked on mine. "You want me to pierce your clit?"

"Yes," I gasp as he pulls me down hard onto his cock. "I want you to pierce my clit, Brick. And then I want you to fuck me like you hate me. But only if you promise to kiss it better when you make it hurt."

"I'll always kiss it better," he growls. "I'll always kiss every part of you better that I hurt. And I'll kiss the parts of you that other people hurt, too, to help you heal."

He dips his head and kisses me on my chest, right above my heart. And then he kisses me gently on the forehead. "I'm going to take away all your bad pain, my Angel. And then I'm definitely going to fuck you like I hate you, until your knees are weak. I can promise you that."

CHAPTER EIGHTEEN

Angel

Later that day

"I want to go next," says Aidan, appearing in front of me, lining his cock up against my entrance.

There's no warning as he buries himself deep inside me with one thrust. I cry out as he fills me up while Brick watches. He groans. "Fuck, Angel. You're always so fucking wet for me. Always ready for me to fill you up."

I rake my nails down his back, scratching him. "Do you remember?" I whisper, thinking back to when we first met.

"I remember," he whispers back.

"The car."

He nods.

"I knew you'd put your nails on me this way," he says, adding more power to his thrust as I dig my nails in even harder.

For once, I want to mark *him*, mark all of them. Show the world they're mine.

He groans and buries his head in the curve of my neck and he nips at me playfully, and then sucks my flesh gently between his teeth. I guess he wants to mark me too, and that's totally fine with me. I'm proud to be his. Proud to be all of theirs.

"Do you want me to fuck you harder, baby?" he rasps as he rolls his hips and thrusts in and out of me.

I nod, breathless. "Mmhmm, yes! Harder, baby!"

He rails me, and I dig my nails deep into his back again, raking them down firmly and feeling his skin catch underneath the edges. He drives into me repeatedly, and the couch squeaks against the floor in response to the power of his thrusts as he impales me with his iron-hard cock over and over again.

As he slams into me, Brick appears beside me, and I turn my face toward him. He dips his head, bringing his mouth to mine and slipping his tongue inside. He crushes his lips against mine, muffling my cries as Aidan continues to plow into me.

"Have you ever fucked two guys at the same time before, Angel?" Aidan's breath is ragged, and his eyes bore into mine as he bites his bottom lip. His gaze trails over my body, watching my tongue wrestle with Brick's.

"No, but I've definitely fantasized about it," I pull my mouth away from Brick's to reply, a shiver of pleasure rushing through me at the thought. Who hasn't wanted to be railed by two hot men at the same time?

"You want to try it now?" Aidan rasps. "Brick's cock buried in your pussy while I fuck you in your tight little asshole?"

"Mmhmm," I moan, my pussy clenching at the thought of being double-penetrated by these two men.

"Good, because that's what we want, too," he growls. "Don't we, Brick?"

Brick nods enthusiastically, feasting on me with his gaze, reaching out to caress one of my breasts as he bites his lower lip.

"Have you two done this before?" I ask. I'm curious, not that it matters if they have or not. They're mine now, and that's what I'm focused on.

They glance at each other as I slide myself off Aidan's cock.

"Not quite like this," growls Brick. "And not with somebody as sexy as you."

"Are you ready for this, Angel?" Aidan asks.

"Yes," I moan.

"Are you sure you're okay?" Brick peers at me, wanting to be sure.

"Yes," I say, more firmly. "I want to do this. How many times do I have to say it?"

He laughs and puts his hands up in mock defense. "Okay, okay. We just want to make sure. This is kind of a big deal."

I nod. "That's fair. And I'm more than ready."

"Slide onto my cock," Brick says, and my pussy clenches as I look at his rock-hard cock, standing at attention, waiting for me to lower myself onto it. I eagerly move forward, straddling him and lining myself up over his tip. I reach down, grabbing his shaft and slowly lower myself onto him. I moan as he fills me up, stretching my walls. His cock is massive, and I'm a little grateful Aidan chose Brick to take my pussy this time, and let himself have my ass. Their cocks are both a decent length and gorgeous, but Brick's is more girthy, and while I'm sure I could get it all the way there, it would be a struggle to take all of him in my ass.

I lower my pussy onto Brick's hard cock, rocking my hips and squeezing myself around him. He groans, his eyes rolling back in his head as I grind against him.

"Fuck, your pussy feels so good wrapped around my cock," he growls. "But you need to wait so that you don't make me explode inside you before Aidan joins our fun." He holds my hips down firmly, stopping me from grinding on him.

I pout. "But your cock feels so good. I want to ride you."

"Be patient and you'll get a chance to ride two of us at the same time," he says, gesturing toward Aidan, who I can see is rock hard as well. "Isn't that what you want?"

I nod, closing my eyes as I think about how it's going to feel having both of them at once. It most certainly is what I want.

Brick rolls both of my nipples between his thumbs and forefingers, and I moan as a ripple of pleasure shoots from the center of my nipples down to my core. My pussy clenches around him involuntarily.

"Hey, I told you to wait," he says, his voice husky.

"You did that to me," I say, gesturing at my tits, which are still cupped by his powerful hands. "I can't help it."

He sucks one of my nipples into his mouth, tugging it gently between his teeth, and I involuntarily clench again. He gives me a warning look. "What? You did that again. It's all you," I laugh. He smacks me on my ass and grabs one of my cheeks hard.

"Stay still, you brat," he growls.

Aidan pops open a bottle of lube, and Brick lies down on his back, pulling my chest against his. I gasp as cold gel hits the top of the seam of my ass. It begins a slow descent, helped along by Aidan's fingers as he uses a finger to rub the lube over my asshole.

Brick reaches behind me and grasps my hair with one hand, pulling my mouth to his, while his other arm wraps tightly around my back. I swipe my tongue through his lips to meet his, and I moan as he sucks on the tip.

I gasp as Aidan slips a finger into my ass, enjoying the cool feeling of the lube.

"You okay, Angel?" asks Brick.

"Yeah, it's just been a while," I say. It didn't feel unpleasant, just something I'm not very used to, although I have had some action back there before. Never with two guys at once, though. This is new. A shiver of pleasure runs through me and I clench against Brick again.

"Watch it," he half-laughs, half-growls. "I told you to wait until he's inside you, too."

"Sorry," I say, not really sorry at all. "I was just imagining what it's going to feel like with my pussy clamped around your cock, and my ass around his, while you both fuck me."

This time I feel Brick's cock twitch inside me.

"Who's unable to control themselves now?" I wink at him and he narrows his eyes at me.

"I'm going in," says Aidan. "You sure you're ready for this?"

"I'm sure." I inhale deeply as he inserts the rest of his finger as far as it can go, and slowly slides it in and out. I feel my walls gripping his knuckle. "Jesus, you're tight back here," he says. "I can barely get one finger in and out, let alone my entire cock."

His finger manipulating the walls of my ass is sending many pleasurable and new sensations throughout my body and I keep clenching on Brick.

"Angel, I told you," Brick groans. "You need to stay still or I'm going to come before Aidan gets anywhere near you with his dick."

"I'm trying not to move," I gasp. "But he's doing things to me with his finger. I can't help it!"

Aidan laughs and leans forward, swiping the hair away from the side of my face and tugging my earlobe gently with his teeth. "You like me finger fucking your ass while Brick has his cock buried deep inside you, don't you, baby?"

"Yes," I moan, my breath quickening.

He slowly extracts his finger from my asshole, and I feel him line his cock up at my back entrance. "How about this?"

"Yes, please," I pant.

"Hold her still, Brick," says Aidan. "Otherwise she's going to bounce around on you and you'll come before I get anywhere near being inside her."

Brick pulls me to him, ensnaring me in his arms and immobilizing me. I enjoy the feeling of being restrained and being completely under their control.

"You doing okay, Angel?" he whispers. I nod, still panting, eager to feel Aidan's hardness inside me at the same time as Brick.

"I'm going to take things slow," growls Aidan, and I nod. "Just try to relax," he says, squeezing my shoulders from behind. "It'll be easier to move once I'm fully inside you."

He slides himself into me. The motion stings and stretches me, but it feels enjoyable as his cock makes its way into my asshole.

"Fuck! I can barely get in you!" he rasps, continuing to work his way in. "You've got a really tight ass. Did you know that?"

"Kiss me and relax your body," says Brick, pulling me to him. His tongue explores mine, distracting me, and I will my entire body to relax and become malleable.

Aidan seizes the moment and slides deeper into me, burying himself deep inside my asshole. I moan as I realize both guys are up to their hilts inside me, stuffing my body with their hard cocks.

I feel my entire body clench, my pussy and ass trapping their shafts, and they both groan under the vice-like grip my body is delivering.

"Jesus, Angel! How the fuck can your body be so tight?" grinds out Brick.

"You think her pussy's tight?" Aidan rasps through gritted teeth. "You should feel her ass. I think she's going to sever my dick in a minute."

It makes me laugh just a little, and that causes me to clench around them some more.

"Fuck!" yells Aidan. "You're so fucking tight. I can't even move! Stop laughing, it makes it worse!"

I pull myself together, taking a deep breath and willing my body to further relax.

"So, are you two going to fuck me or what?" I ask.

Brick's eyes burn dark with lust, and Aidan groans behind me.

"Alright, let's do this," grits out Brick.

They move their hips and quickly find their rhythm, synchronously stroking my pussy and my ass with their deliciously hard cocks.

I lean forward and my tongue swirls with Brick's. He moans as I wrap mine around his, wrestling for a deeper kiss. Aidan reaches around from behind and cups my breasts, letting his fingers trail around their outside curves and then down my back. As he continues thrusting his cock into my ass, he leans forward and kisses me on my upper back.

These two hot men, both inside me at the same time, have me so close to my peak, little bolts of electricity shooting around my entire body. I feel stuffed in a pleasurable way. It's an incredible sensation, like nothing I've ever felt before.

"I'm getting close," pants Brick. "She's fucking milking me."

"Same," grinds out Aidan as he continues to work his way in and out of my ass.

I tilt my hips ever so slightly so that my clit rubs against Brick. I cry out as the combination of their two cocks and the slightest pressure on my clit sends me over the edge, an orgasm ripping through me, my pussy and ass clamping down on both of them at once. My thighs tremble violently as my body seizes around the two cocks buried deep inside me, little fireworks going off in my head, my back arching against Aidan. "Brick, Aidan. Fuck!"

"Fuck!" Aidan cries out as he releases in my ass, and I rear back as I feel his seed shooting deep inside me. My body seizes against both of them, this time sending Brick over the edge, and he climaxes with a roar.

"Angel!" Brick groans as he spills inside me.

Both of their cocks twitch within me and I continue to clench down, milking them as my body trembles.

"Jesus fucking christ," rasps Aidan, kissing me on my back as he carefully slides out of me, his cock beginning to soften. "You're amazing. I really thought I was going to have no dick left after that."

I laugh.

Brick lowers me onto his chest and kisses me gently. "You really are incredible, Angel. I don't know how we got so lucky."

"I'm the one who got lucky," I say softly, wrapping my arms around him and laying my head on his shoulder while Aidan wraps his arms around me from behind.

We lay there for a while, slippery with a combination of my arousal and their cum and our combined sweat. I have never felt more attractive, more empowered and confident than I do right now, sandwiched between these two men.

A moment later, footsteps approach from the kitchen and Slade and Roman enter the room, returned from their outing.

"Well, what do we have here, Slade?" asks Roman rhetorically. "I don't want to jump to conclusions, but it looks a lot like some double penetration just went down. What do you think?"

"Yeah, that's what it looks like to me, too," says Slade, nodding and smirking at me as I lay book-ended by his two friends. "Next time I want to join in."

"Me too," says Roman. "Maybe all five of us can play." A devious grin breaks out across his face and despite having just orgasmed, my pussy twinges at the thought.

"How was it?" asks Slade, his gaze meeting mine. "Did you enjoy having Brick buried in your cunt while Aidan fucked you in the ass, you dirty girl?"

He and Roman are both visibly rock hard through their pants after seeing us like this, and thinking about what just took place.

"It was the fucking best," I say, feeling dreamy, as if I'm floating. "I can't wait to do it again."

The guys glance at each other and smile back at me.

I have the sense their plans for me have only just begun.

And I'm perfectly okay with that.

Chapter Nineteen

Aidan

"Well, well, well. If it isn't the Lost Boys."

I wonder how many times we're going to do this, complain about our frustrations with each other without reaching any real resolution. We're just so different in our approaches to business, our philosophies generally opposed. I don't see room for compromise. But it also feels like we can't go on like this. It's too much of a distraction, probably for them, too.

I kneel, poised over Zeke, knife to his throat.

Rake has Roman in a headlock.

Brick is kneeling on Skyler's chest.

Dom has Slade in a choke hold.

This is a mess.

Zeke's eyes are locked with mine. He doesn't flinch or try to fight me, just stares at me. I have to give him some credit. Most guys would have pissed themselves in this situation. They usually do, turning into crying, whimpering little babies. But Zeke is holding his own. He'll die for his brothers if he has to.

"Just fucking do it, Aidan," he rolls his eyes. "What's the hold-up? Too chicken to slice me from ear to ear?"

"Don't tempt me," I growl.

"Let me guess," he says. "You're running through all the potential scenarios, trying to figure out whether killing me now or later is more beneficial? Assessing the risk?"

"I'm pretty sure it doesn't matter when I kill you, just that I do," I reply, matter-of-fact. He doesn't need to know that he read me accurately just now, articulating exactly what was going through my mind.

"You know I'm right, though," he says, his eyes seeing right through me. "You're paralyzed by analysis. I know you are, because I'm that way, too. Just ask any of my brothers." His eyes flick around to Skyler, Dom and Rake.

I glance down at him and arch an eyebrow. "I have a sharp knife pressed to your throat and you're trying to have a heart-to-heart with me to find all our common ground? That's cute."

He narrows his eyes at me. "You seem a bit more rational than, uh…" His eyes flick over toward the others. "I don't think I'd still be alive if your buddy Brick was the one with the knife."

I smirk. "Oh, he'd probably just knock you out and drag you back to his basement for his kind of fun. A spot of torture to pass the time." I shrug. "We might still decide to do that. We'll just have to see."

Zeke sighs and subtly shakes his head. It's like he's given up for now.

Keeping the knife to his throat, I glance at Brick and Roman.

Rake still has Roman in a headlock, and he's cackling as he messes up Roman's hair. "Take this, pretty boy!" he says as he tousles the top of his head. Roman writhes against Rake's forearm, but he refuses to let go. "You're lucky I don't have a pair of scissors or a razor blade!"

I snort. "Your boy's rearranging my brother's hair."

"Fucking idiot," Zeke shakes his head again casually, as if he doesn't have a knife pressed to his throat. The sharp blade nicks him and a little trickle of blood releases from his neck, but he doesn't seem to notice. "This is how he is unsupervised."

I glance at Brick and Skyler. They're wrestling each other, both full of energy. Skyler flipped Brick off him and now Brick is trying to flip him back over. Brick's clearly in peak wrestling phase. This has come after nunchucks, a flail, and most recently a spear. It feels like Skyler's getting off lightly with this one, the risk of grievous bodily harm still very much there, but reduced drastically without the industrial metals and spikes that Brick's recently been experimenting with.

"Wait!" Angel's voice rings out in the crisp evening air. The wrestling match pauses, everyone stopping momentarily.

"What the fuck are they doing here?" Slade growls, his voice projecting despite Dom still having his forearm wrapped tightly across his throat.

"Fucking hell," says Dom. "Women fuck up everything."

"Stop!" Devon runs to catch up with Angel and they stand in front of us, side-by-side, illuminated by the light overhead, casting shadows of both of them that make their legs appear extra long.

"You shouldn't be here," I yell. "And why are you together? That's weird!"

"He's right. Go home, both of you," calls Zeke, my knife still pressed to his throat.

"We're not going anywhere," yells Devon.

Angel clears her throat. "Don't you see what's happening here? You're tearing each other apart. You're doing exactly what Tane Brown wants you to do. You're doing his bidding and then cutting down anyone else who comes close to being as strong as you. All that does is make him stronger, and it thins the herd, just the way he wants it."

Devon takes her turn to speak. "Instead of fighting each other, what if you leveraged your respective strengths and joined forces? Then you might actually stand a chance of taking control of the island. But this?" she gestures at the eight of us poised to inflict grievous bodily harm on each other, maybe worse. "This is just Tane Brown getting his way. This is you getting in your own way. You may as well hand him the keys to the island and fly to the mainland with your tails tucked between your legs."

The eight of us guys look at each other. What nonsense are these women talking? Since when did they join forces and tell us what to do?

Angel nods. "She's right. So quit it. Stop this stupid fighting and call it a day."

"Since when did you two get along?" Slade yells. "This seems like bullshit to me. Stop trying to distract us when we're focusing on…" he looks around at everyone, "business."

"Since we agreed you were all acting like a bunch of idiots," says Devon, and Angel nods in agreement. "Since we could see that together you have so much potential, that you might actually stand a chance to get what you want. But instead, you're all about to sacrifice everything you've worked so hard for."

"You want us to work together with this bunch of Peter Pan man-children? That think they'll never get old because they have some fucking good energy from the island or whatever?" Slade scoffs.

"And you want us to work with this group of jackholes who came over from the mainland and started twirling their tiny dicks around, taking everything over in their sight and fucking us over in the process?" Skyler snarls. "I'd rather be a Peter Pan than a fucking boring wannabe big shot dude who wears suits every day and discusses stock market derivatives over breakfast."

"I care about you four very much," Angel indicates to me, Slade, Brick and Roman. "I admire your tenacity and ambition to grow your business. I don't think you're boring, you're just… focused. You're mature, but it's not like you're yelling at kids to get off your lawn." She pauses and glances at Slade. "I'm sure Slade would, if you had a lawn, but you know what I mean."

I glance at Slade and Roman and Brick, small smiles spreading across each of our faces. I know they're thinking the same as me, that it's nice to hear Angel sticking up for us, speaking to our character, especially among this group.

"And I love each of you," Devon glances at Skyler, Zeke, Rake and Dom. "Especially how you're all young souls, full of joy and mischief, even when fucked up shit is happening. I don't want to grow old before my time, and you keep me feeling young and satisfied."

Her four men grin at each other.

"Across this group, you have two strong women who love you," says Angel, her eyes narrowing at all eight of us. "So get the fuck over yourselves and your misplaced pride. Stop jockeying for position against each other. The energy is misplaced. You both have a legitimate and important place on this island, and with your combined skills, you actually stand a chance. You might still need help from others when it comes down to it, but the eight of you are exponentially more powerful than four and four separately. Or after the way you were going, like two and two."

They both roll their eyes at us.

"Jesus, they're like the twins in *The Shining* now. I preferred it when they hated each other," says Slade.

I snort at the mental image.

"Listen, I don't like it any more than the rest of you," I say, running my free hand through my hair. "But I think they're right."

"Me too," says Zeke, eyeing the blade in my hand still pressed to his flesh.

I roll my eyes. "For fuck's sake. You'd better know what you're talking about," I call out to Angel and Devon, and they return my gaze, motionless.

Moving my blade away from Zeke's throat, I stand and extend my forearm to him. He takes it and I help pull him up to his feet.

"You were never going to stab me, bro," he says, twisting to shift his back and shoulders into place.

"It was close," I shrug. "I would have if I needed to. You know how it goes."

"Yep," he says, nodding. "Sure do. So we're really partners now?" We stand side by side and survey the scene.

"I guess so," I reply. "Well, that sounds fucking weird, doesn't it?"

He smirks. "Yeah, really fucking weird. Like we're in a parallel universe or some shit. I never would have believed this would ever happen. Still kind of don't. But Devon and Angel sure are something special."

"They sure are," I sigh.

Rake gives Roman's hair one final tousle and then lets him out of his headlock. Roman raises himself up to full height and scowls at Rake. "No hard feelings, man. I'm sorry I fucked with your hair."

"All good, man," says Roman, smoothing his locks into place as much as he can without a mirror.

Dom begrudgingly releases Slade from his chokehold. He and Slade stand next to each other, both scowling.

"Oh my god, you have a grumpy one as well," I say to Zeke.

He laughs. "Yeah, he's our household curmudgeon."

Rake and Skyler help each other up. They're both covered in dirt after their wrestling scuffle. Skyler shakes his head at Brick. "You're one fucking weird dude, man. But you know how to fight. So I respect you."

Brick beams as if it's the nicest compliment he's ever received.

"Should we talk this through now?" Zeke asks, glancing at me. He looks exhausted.

"You know, it's been a big day," I say. "There's still a lot to process, to get our heads around. Why don't we call it a night and then regroup in the morning? We have a lot to discuss."

He nods and we head out. Ten people splitting into two groups of five, heading off in opposite directions.

"Am I still a distraction?" Angel asks Slade as we climb into our vehicle.

"Yes, a massive distraction. But you might have saved a few of us from serious injury tonight. Maybe even saved some lives. So, just this once, I'm going to let it slide," he replies.

Chapter Twenty

Slade

"But if we go into partnership with them, we lose some of our power. Plus, we'd lose our percentage of their take. It's been quite lucrative." I'm very concerned about the proposition to partner with the snakes. I don't feel comfortable needing to trust another group of people, particularly a group that we've had problems with since we moved to the island.

"That profit share was never intended to be permanent, you know that," says Aidan. "Besides, they've already paid off most of their debt. Taking down Tane would be worth so much more."

"It might also cost a lot more," Brick says, and Roman nods. They're both just as concerned as I am.

Aidan shrugs. "That's a risk I'm willing to take if it means getting him off our backs and taking more control."

"We'd have to split that power with them, though," I say. "Divide it amongst us. I don't think we should dilute our control."

"Nah, man, we need to collectively magnify our power," replies Aidan. "Otherwise, we don't have a shot of overthrowing Tane. He's just too strong. It's hard to say after everything we've been through, but we need them. From my point of view, there are no other options."

The three of us look at each other, then back at Aidan, and nod. We know that without a doubt, Aidan's run through many more scenarios than any of us could ever have considered. His logic is consistently sound, and we trust his judgement. Even when it makes us uncomfortable.

I guess that's part of what loyalty is about, believing that someone has your best interests at heart, even when their path to get there isn't what you might have chosen yourself.

Chapter Twenty-One

Angel

"I can't believe we got them to meet, here, on neutral ground." Devon gestures around the Airbnb we've rented for the night.

We both laugh, because the whole situation is just surreal.

I nod. "I know, right? The owners were really skeptical when we said what we wanted to use the space for. They made us give them a chunky deposit in case there's a brawl and the place gets destroyed. Nearly everyone on this island knows our guys don't get along."

Somehow, Devon and I have convinced the guys that they needed to meet and more formally align on some sort of truce. We truly believe that if they join forces, they'll be many steps closer to taking over control from Tane. Through our powers of persuasion combined, we're all in the same building, under one roof, and talking logistics for how the partnership will work in practice.

While things were a little tense at first, after a few tough conversations and cracking some beers open together over a meal, the guys seem to be finding they have more in common than they originally thought.

Not that they want to be best buddies suddenly or anything.

But they might be a wee bit less likely to shoot each other on sight if they end up in the same place at the same time.

They may even be capable of having a civil, amicable conversation.

We glance over at the men, all eight of them, and look back at each other.

"How'd you get yours to agree?" Devon arches an eyebrow.

"I took your advice and found a way to persuade them," I grin. "There was definitely something in it for me, too." I wink and wiggle my eyebrows, and she laughs.

"Nice," she smiles. "I'm glad I could be helpful." She looks across at the guys, who are deep in conversation. "You know, aside from all the craziness, and maybe even because of it, I feel like both of us really are living our best lives," she says, smiling in their direction.

"Most definitely because of it," I say, smiling at them as well. "I wouldn't have it any other way."

CHAPTER TWENTY-TWO

Angel

I quietly close the front door behind me and walk outside. Because it's early, the air is crisp and refreshing, my favorite time to be outside on the island before the humidity and heat build, and before the island really wakes up.

I'm dressed simply in a cropped tank top and bike shorts, with sneakers with heels that are slightly raised. They're ideal for this type of activity, because I'm going to need comfortable footwear for what I have planned.

My vibrant purple hair cascades around my shoulders. Even though it's not sunny out yet, I wear a cap that matches the rest of my outfit and my headphones hold it down firmly in case there is an unforeseen gust of wind. I feel empowered and beautiful, like I can be unapologetically me now.

As I head out down the long driveway and onto the sidewalk, I turn right. My pace is brisk. I've always been a fast walker, and for me, walking is a source of joy. Not consistently being able to walk fast here is something I've had to get used to on the island, especially when I head over to the more populated beach areas where tourists are leisurely enjoying their vacation, wanting to take it slow as they travel on foot from point A to point B.

My naturally brisk pace means that this early hour is the perfect time for me to be taking a walk. It's a precious moment in the day before I'll need to regularly pause and wait for tourists as they dawdle and leisurely stroll along the pavement in the heat of the day. I have to remind myself that their pace is what's considered normal. That my almost breakneck walking speed is what's freakish and not in keeping with island time.

I don't really have a destination in mind. I just want to luxuriate in the fact that I'm able to be outside. My psycho stalker of more than half of my life is finally dead! I'm free, and I want to savor the ability to be in control of my life for once.

While I'm not sure exactly what's ahead, I have the opportunity to shape a beautiful life for myself. The guys seem to want me to stay, to consider me part of their chosen family now. While I have some lingering concerns, I am no longer afraid that they're going to kill me in the imminent future just for existing. Even Slade. Even though I witnessed Roman murder someone with a pair of my hairdressing shears.

I think by now they're all confident that I will not run to the police to snitch on Roman. There would be no benefit in me doing so, and our bond is too great now. I really have fallen for all four of them, and I see a future with them as long as they'll have me.

The air has a briny quality to it as I stalk along the pavement. I slip my headphones on and turn up a fast-paced house track that matches my walking speed. It's so energizing not having to worry about being terrorized by that psycho madman. Brett Wolf is gone for good, just a series of memories and the odd nightmare now.

I walk and enjoy the thumping music for what must be about an hour, just as an estimate. Every step I take is empowering, and I intend to enjoy every moment. It doesn't really matter how long I'm out for now, because there's no need to rush back and lock myself inside in case my stalker stumbles upon me.

After a while, I glance around and seem to be in a different neighborhood, a couple over from the compound. I don't recognize this part of town. What started off relatively industrial has gotten more sparse in terms of buildings. Things are more spaced out, a few abandoned vehicles here and there.

The energy has changed a little, although I can't put my finger on it. Maybe I shouldn't walk alone with my headphones blaring, but for the most part this island is meant to be pretty safe. Especially considering we've gotten rid of my life's primary threat. But I feel a little twinge of something in the nape of my neck and the pit of my stomach—I guess it could be a gut feeling, or maybe I'm just paranoid. I haven't been this far away from the guys since they took me captive. Maybe it's that.

I glance around and pull my headphones off my ears out of an abundance of caution. I hear nothing except for the tweeting sound of birds and the hum of traffic on the freeway off in the distance.

I continue to walk, placing my headphones back on, shrugging off the sense of unease. I get to not feel afraid now. He's gone, and I should be able to walk around wherever I want now. He doesn't get to keep his fear hold over me from beyond the grave. I crank the music back up and continue to walk.

That's when I feel the distinct rumble of an approaching vehicle nearby. I glance around again, and there's nobody else in sight. A large SUV makes its way slowly toward me from one end of the street. I look to see if there are any side alleys or other exits, just in case. I'm probably being silly, but it's always good to have a backup plan. In this case, there isn't one.

There's a chain fence topped with barbed wire to my left, about ten feet high, and even with my sensible sneakers, there's no way I'm scaling that. The other side of the road has an industrial building that spans the block. Signs prominently display 'Keep out' and 'Guard dogs, beware'.

The SUV continues to approach. It's probably nothing, just a coincidence a vehicle is in the neighborhood. It's weird I haven't encountered more people out and about on this refreshing morning. Everyone sleeping in is missing out on the beauty of this golden hour.

I'm sure I'm just still incredibly paranoid after all that's happened recently. Surely that's normal?. But I'm feeling afraid. I should have just stayed at home. But no, I should be able to be out here. Why am I like this?

The shiny white SUV rumbles up and pulls to a stop beside me. The windows are heavily tinted and I can't see inside, but then the windows roll down and I see three goon-like figures look out at me simultaneously. They're all large men, and they look tough. Why are they stopping beside me?

The one in the passenger seat smirks. "Need a ride, love?"

"No—no thank you," I say, quickly. "I'm just enjoying a walk. Thank you. Have a nice day." I continue walking and pick up the pace even from my normal rapid walk.

The SUV follows along beside me, keeping pace with me. "Oh, I should be more clear. We'd like to give you a ride, dear," the man says. "In fact, we insist on it."

My blood chills, and I feel goosebumps across my body.

Instinctively, I pivot and break out into an all-out run in the opposite direction, toward the compound. I've never been a super-fast runner, but I give it my all. My chest pounds and I gasp for air as I run back in the direction I came. I know the car is faster than me, but if I can just find an alleyway to shoot down, somewhere to at least hide while I figure out the next steps, then I should be able to get to freedom. The freedom that I have so desperately craved and finally thought I had in my grasp.

The road is uneven, little pieces of gravel and potholes in the sidewalk's asphalt. A couple of times I trip and once I awkwardly turn my ankle, but I keep going. I hear the SUV turning around in the distance. It sounds like they're taking their time to do some type of three-point turn, not rushing to flip their vehicle around and pursue me. Maybe this will give me the break I need. Maybe this is my chance to get away or at least find a suitable hiding place while I figure out my next steps.

I should call the guys. I should use the phone they gave me to get their help. But I can't stop running or they'll almost certainly catch back up to me.

I reach into my fanny pack and pull out my phone. I try not to slow down as I open the display using Face ID and almost trip on a bump on the uneven sidewalk, but manage to rebalance myself at the last second. Relieved, I pull up my contacts and dial Slade, who shows up first on my recently called list.

I put the phone to my ear as I continue to race away from the SUV and toward the compound. By now, I can hear the vehicle rumbling toward me again, slowly now, as if taunting me. As if they know my heart is about to burst out of my chest and my running stamina is not that great and I'm feeling a searing pain in my shins. I'm not used to the pressure of my legs slamming down on the pavement with force. I may be a fast walker but definitely not used to urban running, or any running for that matter. I'm not built for this.

Slade answers on the second ring. "Angel, where are you?" He sounds confused. "Why are you calling... from the other side of the house?"

"I—," I pant, gasping for breath and struggling to get the words out. "I went for a walk."

"You left?" His confusion turns to concern. "We told you not to, Angel. It's danger-ous."

My chest is searing as I struggle to breathe and talk. I can feel the SUV getting closer. "I— I needed to. I needed fresh air," I explain, my words coming out ragged. "He's dead. I thought it would be okay."

I need to stop for a second to gasp for air.

"Well, we can talk about that later, but are you okay?"

"No, there's... an SUV... following me. They insisted... I get in... their car." I keep moving, focusing carefully on the uneven sidewalk to avoid tripping again or twisting my ankle.

"What color is it, Angel?" Slade asks. "What type of SUV?"

I picture the vehicle with the windows rolled down and the goons looking out. "White with chrome wheels and tan upholstery, from what I could see."

"Which way did you go on your walk?" he asks.

By now, even though it's moving slowly, the SUV is almost right alongside me. Despite the heat I'm generating from my pace, I feel the shackles of my neck sticking up, icy goosebumps covering my body. I can almost feel the breath of the goons on me from the vehicle. I glance furtively left and right but still don't see any opportunity to dart away. Fuck.

"I... turned right.... out of the house. Kept walking... maybe an hour... I walk fast. Don't know.. this area. Industrial.... less populated."

"Okay, Angel," says Slade, his voice low. "Try to stay calm. Is there a way you can get off the road?"

"Don't... see... there are fences and buildings. Not any... alleys."

The SUV is fully alongside me now. The windows roll down again and I see the three goons all watching me. I gasp as the vehicle comes to a complete stop. The three men get out and approach me.

"They're... here. Can't... keep running." My chest is heaving, and I'm embarrassed as tears flow involuntarily from both of my eyes. This can't be happening. Just one walk, one taste of freedom, is all my soul craved. All I needed. It seemed like a small ask, inconsequential. But now I'm not so sure. What have I done?

The men flank me, and I know there's nowhere for me to run now. Especially after all the running I've already done. I'm exhausted.

"Hand us the phone," the guy from the passenger side of the vehicle says, extending his hand.

I comply, not seeing any other options than throwing it on the floor, which would seem to be counterproductive.

He takes it from me and puts it to his ear. "And who do I have the pleasure of speaking with today? One of the Brixtons, I presume?"

I can't hear Slade on the other end of the phone, but by the look on the goon's face, I am sure he's on the receiving end of a volley of expletives. He smirks. "Yes, we'll be taking Angel with us now. We'd like to negotiate a little redistribution of assets and control on this island. We will send further instructions. In the meantime, we're going to take her away, maybe have a little fun with her."

This time, I hear yelling from the other end of the line. I can't make out the words, but I know they're not polite. Suddenly, the noises stop and there's a feeling of calm.

I can almost imagine Aidan soothing Slade in the background, reminding him that responding in this way might cause these guys to hurt me more than they might already be planning to. Ice-cold fear grasps my heart, but there's also a sliver of warmness and familiarity as I see this scene playing out in my head. But just as quickly as it began, that thought is yanked away as the man growls into the phone.

"We will send further instructions. Do exactly what we say, or your precious girl dies." He ends the call and the three men circle me.

Then I feel a prick of pain in my neck from behind, and my vision blurs.

Fuck my life.

Not again.

Chapter Twenty-Three

Roman

"She went for a fucking walk?" I rub my hand over my eyebrow and one of my eyes. "You have to be fucking kidding me."

"I guess she thought she was safe with her stalker gone," sighs Slade. "I don't think she realized the gravity of what living with us means. That it puts a target on her back from a range of other players trying to take over our turf."

"We need to save her and kill these fuckers," growls Brick, cracking his knuckles, his breathing audible and aggressive.

"Obviously, yes to all the above," says Aidan. I know what's coming. He's going to tell us we need to do it in a sensible way that keeps everyone as safe as possible. And then Brick and Slade will complain but eventually comply.

"Let's think this through first, not do anything rash that might compromise her safety."

Brick and Slade sigh simultaneously. Bingo. Not hard to psychoanalyze this little group. Or maybe it's just because we all know each other so well, we've fallen into these patterns.

"So what's the plan?" I ask.

"They said to await further instructions, so I think we should do that. It sounds like we were speaking with Swarenski's men, based on Angel's description of the SUV, as well as the brief exchange with one of the guys."

"They are all from here, right? Originals from the island?"

"Yeah," sighs Aidan, running his hand through his hair. "That's exactly right. And you know who knows them well?"

"Those fucking snakes," growls Slade.

"You're saying they might actually come in useful for something for once?" asks Brick, raising an eyebrow.

"That would be a fucking first. About time, though," Slade sneers.

"I think that's our best shot," nods Aidan. "Roman, would you like to do the honors, or should I?"

"I'll give Skyler a call," I reply, sighing. "I don't like the guy very much, but I think I can get through to him."

I dial his number, and he picks up on the third ring. "Roman?"

"Yeah, it's me, Roman." I take a deep breath and steel myself. I don't enjoy asking for favors. "Listen, we need your help."

"Oh you do, do you? That's interesting," says Skyler. "Keep talking."

Chapter Twenty-Four

Angel

Fuck. *Fuck!*

I wake up, and once again I'm not in the location I intended to be. I'm in a dark room, thankfully not shackled this time, but it's cold in here and I can't see shit.

The men on this island really can't seem to stop taking women hostage. Kidnapping them. Holding them captive. Just moving them around on a fucking whim, it seems!

My eyes adjust. It's cool in here, definitely air-conditioned. The room is fairly bland from what I can make out, empty. Four walls and no windows. I try to listen for anything helpful in figuring out where I am, but it's eerily silent.

I'm such an idiot for going for a walk, now that I think about it. So giddy that my psycho stalker was dead that I forgot who I was living with, and what the implications were of living with the Brixton men. They're powerful, successful, and there are other groups that covet their hold on this island. It was complete idiocy of me to forget that just because the man that taunted me for so long was dead, I still need to take safety precautions and not prance around like Miss fucking Independent. I could have taken a guard, but that just seemed so extra.

I just wanted a moment for myself, but now I see why that was a mistake.

A big one.

And now I may have to pay the ultimate price.

CHAPTER TWENTY-FIVE

Roman

Skyler and I agree to regroup half an hour after the initial phone call. He committed to doing some research with his guys and to make some phone calls to figure out what we're really dealing with.

After almost exactly thirty minutes, my phone rings and it's him calling back. I answer on the first ring.

"Yep," I growl into the phone, eager to hear what progress he's made.

"Okay, here's the plan," says Skyler calmly. "Meet us around the corner of the Swarenski compound at 4 o'clock sharp. We're going in together. We know a weak point that should enable us to resolve this fairly quickly."

"You're sure? You think we can get her back this easily?"

"Listen, we have a history with these guys. We're prepared to leverage it to help you rescue your girl. I needed to call in a few favors, but seeing we're going into partnership consider this some type of olive branch."

"Alright," I growl. "But you better not fuck this up."

"Oh we won't," says Skyler. "We're more worried that you will."

Chapter Twenty-Six

Aidan

The eight of us guys stand over six of Swarenski's men. They're pitiful, kneeling down and flinching, protecting their heads and shoulders.

After Skyler gained us access to Swarenski's compound, we were able to pick off most of the guards one by one, and we ended up in the center of the building with these guys, who appear to be the strongest of the group.

"Why are you all cowering? What do you think we are, monsters?" Brick laughs like a maniac. He gestures to Dom. "Did you hear that, man? The sound of silence. They think we're monsters."

"I have no idea why they'd say that," says Dom, picking up one of the two branding irons that's been heating on the coals in front of us, and handing it to Brick. He holds the other one in his left hand.

"Now, how about you start telling us what we need to know." Brick smiles sweetly at the men.

He presses the branding iron into the hand that one man is holding on top of his head to protect his skull. There's a sizzling sound, a little billow of smoke emanating from the metal as it sears into the man's flesh. The man screams. "We're going to mark you all over. Nobody will accept you when we're done, so you may as well tell us what we want to know."

The man stays silent.

"Very well," says Brick. He shrugs, raises his gun and shoots the man in the back of the head.

The other men keep their heads lowered, but they flinch and adjust themselves awkwardly, probably wondering if Brick's about to completely lose it and travel down the line to dish out the same fate.

"This is your last chance, guys," Brick says, and Dom nods in agreement, the two enforcers doing their thing. "Let me help you help us. Tell us where she is."

They move in front of the second guy in the line. "Your turn, sweet pea! Tell us what you know."

The man whimpers as Slade joins Brick and Dom and touches the cold metal of the gun to the man's temple. "Clock's ticking. Tick-tock!"

The man cries out, "I don't know anything! I swear!" but his eyes betray him, darting to the man next to him.

"Maybe my friend Brick here can persuade you otherwise," Slade gestures at Brick, whose face is stony as he eyes up the man.

"I can be very persuasive when I want to be!" shouts Brick merrily.

He extends the branding iron and applies it to the man's cheek. The acrid scent of burning human flesh wafts through the room as the man screams in agony.

"You sound so pretty when you sing like that, dollface," says Brick in a sing-song voice, continuing to hold the iron against his flesh.

The man instinctively goes to grab the hot metal bar and rips his hands away at the agony caused by the molten heat. He whimpers more.

Despite the pain he's experiencing, his eyes point again to the man to his right, as if he's giving us a signal.

Slade moves on to the next man in the line, and Dom and Brick follow.

"What about you, sir? You've got some secrets you'd like to share?" asks Slade, getting into the enforcer role as well. "Information on our girl's whereabouts?"

This man stifles a whimper.

"It's okay to be scared, sweet cheeks," says Brick as he extends the red-hot poker until it's only a couple of inches from this man's eye. He flinches at the heat emanating from the hot metal.

"Start talking," growls Brick.

"I don't know anything," the guy says, his voice cracking.

"I have a real problem with lying," says Slade. "It's the one thing I can't let you off the hook for. I'd say 'you see' but that would be ironic, wouldn't it Brick?"

"Yep, a little too ironic." Brick grins as he stabs the branding iron into the man's eye socket. His eyeball sizzles and a satisfying pop rings out, and I can only assume the little explosion sound was from his eyeball disintegrating under the pressure and the heat.

The man screams and his body bucks as if he's having a seizure, his nerve endings firing all over his body, frantically trying to work out how to battle away this threat.

"Please, please stop!" he shrieks. "I'll tell you everything I know." He holds his hand over his eye and whimpers, fluid oozing to the floor into a puddle below him, a mixture of red and clear goo.

"That's more like it," croons Brick. "Tell us everything. No detail is too small."

The guy starts to speak, his voice coming out in a largely inaudible croak.

"Fucking snitch," the guy next to him interrupts, muttering under his breath.

"Silence!" yells Slade.

"Talk," growl Brick and Dom in unison.

The men refuse to talk. Something in the second man's tone has reminded the now one-eyed man that he made a vow, that there's a cause worth more than his own life.

"Fine, have it your way," sighs Slade, shooting them both between the eyes.

The row of dead men has no more tales to tell. We step over their lifeless bodies as we exit the room. Brick kicks one of them on the way out.

"We're going to get her back. If it's the last thing I ever do, I'm going to see to it that she's safe and away from these guys," huffs Slade.

"And then I'm going to torture them for taking her. I'm going to slice them into tiny little pieces one by one while the others watch," says Slade, his voice a little excited. "There's going to be a lot of basement time for me over the next week."

"I love the sentiment here, guys, but let's make sure we're focused on what needs to happen today, alright?" I need them to focus on the now, not what's happening afterward. We need to be completely focused on what it will take to get her back.

Skyler wasn't wrong. It only takes looking behind a couple more doors to find Angel locked away in a nearly empty room. Swarenski isn't far away, his primary goons no stronger than the six we just took out as they knelt pitifully on the floor.

"No more walks, Angel," Slade growls, wrapping his arms around her protectively after freeing her from captivity.

"No more walks. I get it now," she sighs, no doubt tired of being kidnapped countless times starting with Roman. She's so used to this by now, but I'm really hoping this is the last time.

We were four adversaries away from Tane Brown. Now we're three men away, and although the stakes exponentially increase each time we move up one position, it feels good.

CHAPTER TWENTY-SEVEN

Roman

"Well, we helped you save your woman," says Aidan to Zeke. "And now you've helped save ours. I think I'd call that even."

"I know we make fun of your moral code or whatever you want to call it," says Zeke. "I still don't agree with it, but I kind of understand it. It doesn't mean we'll ever have one, though. Let me make that clear. We'll go where the profits are to be made and where we can build the power."

"That's fine," says Aidan. "You guys do your thing. Hell, we've recently found we're willing to go way outside our boundaries. We'll do anything for Devon, anything to protect our queen." His face darkens as if he's recalling a very unpleasant memory.

"Oh, so you killed for her," nods Brick. "I know that look. The first time I killed someone, it was for a girl, too."

Zeke's face blanches slightly, like he's not proud of whatever happened. "I'm not going into details, but we did what we needed to do."

"Well, it's nice to know you're not a bunch of goody-two-shoes after all," shrugs Slade. "You just need a reason more compelling to you than money or power. We can get behind doing anything to support your woman. We feel the same way about Angel. We'd do anything for her."

Brick nods enthusiastically.

"When we heard you'd entered into this type of relationship, we thought you were copying us," says Skyler. "That because we had it you wanted it, too."

"Actually, it was Angel who saw what you had, the day that she and Devon first clashed and almost scratched each other's eyes out," shrugs Aidan. "I think it helped her to realize the possibilities. Things she might never have considered before."

"Damn, bro," says Rake. "We get credit for saving your girl, and now also for her being your girl. You're going to owe *us* now."

Chapter Twenty-Eight

Angel

Roman knocks on my open door and pops his head into my room. "Angel, we all want to speak with you."

"Um, that sounds ominous." I squint at him. "Are you all still mad that I went for a walk and ended up being kidnapped?"

He shrugs. "It wasn't your best judgement, but we understand and none of us are mad. We're just glad you're back safely."

"Are you sure this isn't going to be about how you all want me to leave because your lives would be far more simple that way?" A frisson of concern shoots through my body, a little knot forming in my stomach. "That you're done with me?"

"No, no," he shakes his head quickly, trying to allay my concern. "It's nothing bad. In fact, we want to clear things up to make sure there's no doubt in your mind about how we all feel about you, individually and collectively."

"Oh, I see. Okay then." Finally, some clarity. Everything's been so organic until now, and I've been trying to go with the flow, to enjoy the moment as much as possible. But it has been hard, not knowing what's going to happen next, not knowing where I stand now that my psycho stalker is dead. I know they all care about me, and I know my relationship with them is strong in many ways, but I've always worried that I'm at risk of being discarded. And at this point, who am I without them? I've been strong, I've been independent, but they've woven themselves into the fabric of my being and I know I'd never be the same without the Brixtons in my life. So some clarity is welcome, even if this type of formal conversation about it is a bit intimidating.

"Meet us in the living room in half an hour, Angel."

"Okay. I'll see you soon."

He kisses me on the forehead and leaves.

I get ready, throwing on shorts and a tank and putting my hair up in a topknot. I put on some foundation and mascara and a slick of eyeliner and dab my lips with a shiny clear gloss. May as well look cute for this serious meeting.

When I get to the living room, they're all waiting for me. They look up as I enter, each of them smiling at me. The air is electric with a sense of expectation that I can't quite put my finger on. At least no-one is frowning or looking concerned. Maybe they do really want me here forever and this is just about logistics.

"Angel, come and take a seat," says Aidan, gesturing to a spot on the couch between him and Roman. I walk over and take a seat, enjoying the feeling of their strong thighs pressed against mine. Brick sits opposite us in the armchair, and Slade sits to the other side of Aidan.

"Listen, we realize that things have been a bit up in the air since... well, since the end of Brett Wolf."

Normally, a shiver would trickle down my spine at the sound of his name, but today I feel nothing. It's just a name now, an unpleasant memory and a sense of closure. I still have some work to do to fully process everything, but I know I'm on the right track.

"We want to let you know where things stand from our perspective, and how we want things to move forward from here."

"That sounds very formal," I say, half-joking.

"Well, here's the thing, Angel. We all care very much about you. We're all infatuated with you. I'll go so far as to say we are all completely in love with you. You've changed every one of our lives since you arrived at this house. We all want you to be here."

I look around at each of the guys and from the expressions in their eyes, I know this is true for all of them. Brick and Roman are nodding, and Slade's historically icy gaze has a surprising and comforting warmth to it, like at least part of him has thawed.

"So we wanted to talk through how this would work in practice. We don't want to set hard rules around who you spend time with and when. That's really not how we operate, and I think you know that."

I nod. I've never felt pressured to spend any time with one or more of them. It's just happened organically, and that's felt good to me.

"But," he says, putting a finger up, "you will belong to all four of us, and only us, if you choose to live under this roof. And we would commit ourselves only to you. You would be ours, Angel, and we would be yours. Do you understand?"

I'm breathless at the thought. These four incredibly hot, amazing men, wanting me. Wanting to be mine and mine alone. "I—yes, that's what I want too, very much." The words come out almost as a loud whisper, the loudest I can muster as I feel myself melting inside.

"It sounds like we should celebrate," grins Brick. "What do you all think?"

Slade grins, and it's even hotter than his resting Slade face, his mouth forming a half-smirk that I haven't seen before. Roman smiles at me, his eyes molten with desire, which takes me back to the time in his room where I dropped my towel and spent the night snuggled in his arms.

Aidan's gaze meets mine, and he doesn't need to say a word to communicate his desire. He places a hand on my thigh and my leg quivers at his touch. I can feel my panties getting saturated, arousal dripping from my core in anticipation of what's about to happen. He dips his head down and his mouth meets mine, the other men looking on as we engage in a passionate kiss, our tongues exploring each other, his hand purposefully trailing up my thigh, his fingers beginning to caress my folds through my clothing.

"We're all overdressed," says Brick. "It's time for a sexy party, and that requires no clothing on Angel."

I snort. Even comments like that couldn't kill the mood right now.

"Lift your arms up," directs Aidan, and I happily comply. He pulls off my shirt and bra, exposing my breasts, and my nipples immediately harden as I feel four pairs of eyes on them. He dips his head down and sucks one of my nipples into his mouth, caressing it with his tongue. I moan as the twirling of his tongue sends a lightning bolt from my nipple straight to my core.

Next thing I know, Slade is kneeling in front of me, and has taken my second nipple into his mouth and is sucking on it.

Aidan gently lifts me up by my hips as Slade continues to suck on my nipple, and slides my shorts and panties off in one movement, leaving me bare. Returning my ass to the couch, he presses his mouth to mine again, and I moan as he slides one of his fingers inside my pussy.

"Jesus, you're so fucking wet, Angel."

"How could I not be, in this situation?" I moan.

Slade looks up from my chest height and smiles at me. His hand is next to Aidan's, and he slides one of his fingers inside me as well. Both men have fingers inside me now, and I gasp as they move them in rhythm. I've never had two men fingering me at the same time before, and it's hot as fuck. I spread my thighs further apart to give them better access and I gasp as they both plunge their fingers in deeper, while Brick and Roman look on, their eyes dark with lust.

Brick moves over directly in front of me. "I need to taste you," he growls. "Do you mind?" He gestures to Aidan and Slade and they move to the side to give him access. He growls again as he presses my thighs apart, his eyes locked on my glistening folds. "Aidan was right. You are fucking soaking, Angel. I can't wait to taste how excited you are."

Grabbing me underneath my ass with his large, powerful hands, he pulls me to the edge of the couch, bringing me right up to his face. Then he dips his head and feasts on my pussy, his tongue exploring every part of me. I moan as he slides it inside me and tongue-fucks me, extracting my arousal and moaning as he savors the taste. Then he turns his attention to my clit, lapping at it while holding me still despite my hips feeling like they want to buck off the couch at his touch. When I'm at the edge of an orgasm, Brick abruptly pulls away.

"Ro, you want to do the honors?" he grins, and Roman wastes no time getting down on his knees in front of me and resuming where Brick left off. His tongue works expertly, too, and he slides two fingers inside me while he twirls it around my clit. In only a moment, I'm at the edge again, and this time I'm allowed to cross right over it, my hips bucking and writhing as my pussy clenches around Roman's fingers as he sucks my clit into his mouth and keeps it there while I come. My eyes roll back and I see stars as I ride the peak, and when the wave of pleasure finally subsides and I refocus my vision, I see the other three men looking on at my legs clamped around Roman's neck, his face still buried in my pussy.

"Mmm, good girl," says Aidan. "Now, sit down on me, Angel."

I turn around, my back to his chest, and straddle him. I lower myself onto his rock-hard cock and he groans.

"Fucking hell, baby," he growls in my ear. "Your tight pussy feels amazing wrapped around my hard cock. Did Roman and Brick make your pussy feel good?"

His husky voice causes my pussy to clench around him even tighter. "Mmhmm, real fucking good," I moan.

"Mind if I join you?" asks Slade.

I bite my bottom lip and beckon him over. "What do you have in mind? My pussy is... taken," I say, as I roll my hips on top of Aidan, grinding down on him.

"Not all of it is taken. And I want to taste you, too," says Slade, getting to his knees and spreading my legs further apart, causing me to sink down further onto Aidan's engorged cock.

He dips his head and licks the lengths of my folds, his deliciously long tongue twirling around my clit and then sucking it into his mouth. He flattens his tongue against my clit and begins lapping at it. My hips buck upward toward his face. I groan as he sucks my clit into his mouth again and lashes it with his tongue, his head bobbing up and down in rhythm with my hips.

"Hold her still," he says to Aidan. "Don't let her move for a moment. I want to torture her with my tongue while she can't move. I want to make her come all over your cock and my face."

"Okay, just keep your tongue away from my dick. She's the only one I want sucking it."

I moan and grind my pussy over Aidan's cock.

Aidan groans, "Oh yeah, baby. I'm so deep inside you." He leans forward and nips me on my upper back. I yelp and clench my pussy around him even tighter.

Aidan does as Slade instructed, grabbing my hips and stilling me so that the only movement is Slade's tongue lapping at my clit. I'm trapped, unable to move as his long tongue strokes against me, teasing me and whipping me into a frenzy. My clit is already sensitive from Brick and Roman's earlier attention, and I moan as he sucks it into his mouth and then nibbles on it, and my pussy seizes even more firmly around Aidan's cock.

He groans loudly. "Fuck. Your pussy is like a vice!". I may not be able to move my hips, but there's nothing stopping me from squeezing against Aidan's iron-hard shaft.

Although I just orgasmed from both Brick and Roman eating my pussy only moments before, my body is thoroughly enjoying Slade's follow-up and it doesn't take me long to get right back to the edge. My pussy clenches repeatedly around Aidan's cock as ribbons of pleasure roll outward from my clit and spread their tendrils throughout my body.

"Jesus, she's milking my cock, man. I don't know how long I can hold on. She's tight as fuck. I can barely move inside her."

He reaches around and cups my breasts, and I moan as he rolls my nipples between his thumbs and forefingers.

"You're so fucking beautiful when you come," says Aidan. "Isn't she, Slade?"

Slade nods, gazing up at me, my arousal slick on his mouth and chin. "Very."

"We're going to make you fall apart for us right here, right now. These are just a couple of the many orgasms you'll be having today. We fully intend to celebrate having you back, every inch of you."

Roman and Brick both surround us, so now I'm flanked by all four men. "Slade needs you, baby," says Aidan. "I do, too. But start off with him and come back to me. I want your ass."

Slade sits on the couch next to us, his rock-hard cock erect and welcoming. I slide myself gently off Aidan and turn to straddle Slade, then I slide my pussy down on Slade's large cock while the others watch.

He groans. "Fucking hell, you're so tight."

I roll my hips and gently slide myself up and down on him as he grabs my hips and helps to control my pace. My lips meet his and our tongues tangle in a passionate kiss as I continue to ride him.

I hear the cap of a lube bottle and my ass instinctively clenches in anticipation. I need to do the opposite, to relax. Because I don't know who intends on fucking my ass, but they're all pretty well endowed and the last thing I need is to tense myself up before they're inside me.

"Are you sure you're ready for this, Angel?" Aidan asks, his eyes dark with lust. "Because I have a feeling once we've had you this way we're going to want it all the time."

"Fuck yes, I want it like this," I moan.

I turn and watch as Aidan squeezes some lube from the tube and rubs it all over his cock. He spreads some onto two of his fingers and smears it over my tight hole, working it into my entrance.

"Hold her still," directs Aidan, and Slade tightens his grip on my hips so that I can't keep riding him. As much as I want to keep slamming myself down on him, I know I need to stop while Aidan also works his way inside me.

Aidan lines his cock up with my asshole and pushes himself in slowly. At first there's resistance and then the lube does its thing and he slides deep inside. I cry out as he buries me to his hilt. It was slippery, but he's still large, still filling up a place in my body that hasn't had a lot of attention before.

"Are you okay, Angel?" he whispers as he cups my breasts from behind, buried inside me.

"Yes, baby," I rasp.

He and Slade are both buried deep inside of me and I feel full, stuffed, and I can't wait to move with them.

I roll my hips, gently at first, while I get a feel for the best angle to accommodate both of their cocks. I tilt my hips and slide up and down and they both groan.

"We're going to fuck you now," says Aidan. "Let us take control."

I still myself, and they thrust into me. They're in sync, but the force is coming from my front and my back in a way that I'm not used to, so it feels unpredictable. I roll with their thrusts and moan as the pressure builds within me, the coil tightening in my core. Aidan reaches around my waist and flicks at my clit with his long, skilled fingers and I moan. My pussy and ass clench in response and they both groan again.

Aidan kisses me on my neck, nipping at me and I giggle, then lean forward and once again entangle my tongue with Slade's.

I've been so mesmerized by what's happening that I almost forgot about Brick and Roman. I glance over to the side. Brick is sitting on the couch, legs apart and cock out, stroking himself.

Roman stands just behind Aidan and gazes as Aidan and Slade bury their cocks deep inside me. He's erect and I can see a bead of pre-cum at his tip.

"Want me to get that for you?" I rasp, and he moves closer to us. His cock ends up being at the same height as my mouth and I lick the pre-cum off the tip.

"Get over here, Brick," I say, and he growls as he stands up and comes over to my other side, where I reach out and touch him with my hand, wrapping my palm around his shaft.

As I continue to ride Slade with my pussy and Aidan with my ass, I stroke my hand up and down Brick's shaft. He groans as I twirl my palm gently.

I slide my lips over Roman's hard cock and suck it into my mouth. He groans as I use my other hand to work his shaft as my tongue swirls around his tip. Continuing to stroke him, I turn my head over to Brick and take him in my mouth now.

"Fuck, Angel, your lips are so fucking perfect on my cock," he groans, thrusting himself into my mouth.

I turn my head again, alternating between him and Roman, continuing to use my hands on both. They roll their hips in rhythm with my hands, which are also in rhythm with the thrusts from both Aidan and Slade. I've never felt so full, so stuffed, so used in the best way. We're like an orchestra, moving together, nobody trying to overtake the other. It's selfless. They're all worshipping me and I am equally attending to each of them.

My body is electric, zaps firing all over me as all four men bury themselves in my holes, a plethora of sensations attacking me at the same time. It's sensory overload and my body tenses up. I can feel the pressure building from my core and radiating outward. My pussy and ass clench around Aidan and Slade and I grip Brick and Roman more tightly, moaning on Roman's cock as an orgasm shatters through my body, pleasure radiating all over me as I ride the wave. They all groan simultaneously and talk dirty as Slade and Aidan come inside me, releasing deep within me. Roman and Brick shoot their seed all over me, splattering my face and neck and chest.

I'm panting, covered in sweat, and they continue to ride out their respective orgasms, my body still wrapped around them all.

Brick leaves the room as Aidan pulls himself out of me and lifts me off Slade. He places me gently on the couch as Brick returns with a wet cloth and gently wipes me down. They all watch me, and they're all glowing like I know I am as well. That was an almost out-of-body experience and I couldn't imagine anything more perfect.

We sit there, together, all five of us, silently for a while. I'm snuggled up against Slade and Roman is on my other side, his hand stroking my thigh. Brick sits at my feet, his head on my leg.

"Let's get you to bed, Angel," says Aidan softly, after a while. He takes me by my hand and guides me to my bedroom, but he doesn't make a move to leave. "I want to lie with you tonight, if that's alright with you," he says.

"So do I," says Roman, his voice appearing from behind us.

I slip into bed and they each get in on either side. My back is to Aidan, and he snuggles up against me like the big spoon. Roman faces me and gently traces his finger along the side of my face, down my jaw.

"You're so perfect," he says. "I love you. We all love you."

Aidan squeezes his arms around me, his way of indicating he agrees.

"I love you too," I whisper. "Both of you. All four of you."

Aidan kisses me on the back of the head and I smile at Roman, my lids heavy in a relaxing and contented way, as I lay in their arms and we drift off to sleep.

Chapter Twenty-Nine

Angel

I look down at my hand, admiring Brick's literal handiwork, now that my tattoo is mostly healed. It's like he took the most beautiful rose and made it even more exquisite somehow. He's an enigma. This stone-cold killer who gets off on torturing people and knife play, but who would never eat an animal and draws the most delicate, intricate body art.

"Brick, thank you," I whisper. "It's the most beautiful tattoo I've ever seen. You're so talented. I can't believe I get to wear this on my hand forever."

"It was an honor to create a design on someone as breathtakingly gorgeous as you. And no matter what you decide to do, you'll have a memory of your strength that will be with you always. And maybe when you look at it, you'll think of me, too."

"Always, Brick," I whisper, slipping my hand into his.

He pulls me close and kisses my forehead. "My sweet Angel, my Valkyrie. I never, ever want to let you go."

I wrap my arms around him. I don't want to let him go, either. I don't want to let any of them go. But I might have to.

CHAPTER THIRTY

Angel

"We want to show you something, baby," says Brick, his eyes gleaming with excitement. "We picked it out just for you."

"Oh yeah? What is it?" I raise an eyebrow. I assume they've probably got me a nice dress or some sexy lingerie to wear for them.

"It's a bit of a drive away. Get ready and come with us."

I get dressed and pull my hair up in a ponytail. It feels like a casual but special occasion, having survived the events leading up to today, so I pull on a simple but elegant black romper that makes me feel cute and sexy. I apply a little tinted moisturizer, lengthen my lashes with mascara, and add a dab of bright pink lip gloss. On my feet I wear some stripy black sandals accented with silver, and I painted my toenails a vibrant pink hue. Assessing myself in the mirror, seeing the sparkle in my eyes, I can see that I look as happy as I feel. It has been a struggle to get to this point, but I've arrived and it feels really fucking good.

The guys all smile at me appreciatively as I descend the stairs. They're patiently waiting for me, nobody calling out to rush me, all perfectly content waiting to do whatever this is on my time.

We all head out of the compound and hop into the SUV. Aidan drives us carefully out of the industrial neighborhood, and onto the highway, where we continue to travel for about half an hour.

"Where are we going?" I ask, unfamiliar with the area we're passing through and seeing no sign of us taking an exit. "This is kinda far."

"It'll be worth it when you see it," says Slade. "Trust us."

I consider his words carefully and come to the conclusion that I really do trust them. It's a weird feeling. Trust. Doesn't feel familiar, but it also feels good with them.

After about five more minutes of driving, we take an exit into a neighborhood that seems to be a bustling combination of high-end apartment buildings and sprawling residential homes, boutique stores, and trendy restaurants and bars. We soon arrive at a standalone building with paper taped over the windows. It's painted cream with black accents, giving away no clue what's inside, although the color palate looks upscale.

Brick blindfolds me with a piece of black silk, and Slade and Roman each take one of my hands and lead me inside.

They carefully guide me several steps inside the entrance and get me to stop, and then they remove the blindfold and instruct me to open my eyes.

I look around the space and gasp as I take it all in.

It's the most beautiful hair salon I've ever seen.

At the entrance, there's an ornate marble desk with a state-of-the-art point-of-sale system to ring up happy clients. A discreet display stands behind it, featuring top-quality hair products that I've always fantasized about having in my salon.

The waiting room features a luxurious tufted couch that I can imagine clients relaxing on while they flick through the generous stack of attractively glossy magazines artfully stacked on the sleek glass coffee table that sits low in front of it.

The hair-washing stations are discreetly tucked away, and the recliners are gorgeously padded white leather armchairs with a massage function. Overhead, chandeliers scatter a warm, twinkling glow throughout the entire space.

Gold-framed mirrors line the walls, and each stylist station has a comfortable swivel chair for clients. Hairdryers and other tools hang on overhead hooks, out of the way and creating a hairstylist chic look.

"Oh my god," I gasp as I soak it all in. "This is the most beautiful hair salon I've ever seen. It's the salon of my dreams."

To the side is an area set up for tattoos. It's black and gold and gorgeous. I recognize the leather recliner from the house. "For me to do guest appearances now and then," Brick explains, beaming. When he was doing my tattoo, I didn't realize how carefully he was listening to what I was saying, how he must have been mentally taking notes that have manifested into noticeable touches throughout this space. My heart flutters as I realize how much he truly sees me, how much he cares. How much they all do.

"Wow, how did you find this place?" I ask. "It's amazing."

"We looked around until we found the place that was perfect for you," smiles Roman, his gaze warm and locked on mine.

"You—you really got this for me?" It doesn't feel real. I feel like the luckiest woman alive. And it's not because of this place. It's because of how these four men collectively make me feel. Seen. Heard. Truly cared for. Like I really belong.

"Yes, it's all yours," says Aidan, beaming at me. "Whether or not you stay with us, we want the best for you, always. Our queen deserves nothing but the best."

"Wow, I don't know what to say." I feel my eyes watering and I blink back the tears. Nobody has ever done anything like this for me. It's so thoughtful and generous. I didn't mind working out of my old salon in the strip mall. It had everything I needed, even though it was basic and not at all fancy. But this is the next level. Not because it clearly wasn't cheap, but because it represents me.

"Just say you want to be with us forever," says Brick, his eyes eager. Then he quickly looks down. "But only if that's true. I know we can't force you to stay. This has to be on your terms, and your terms alone."

Slade clears his throat. "Um, Angel, I have something for you," he says. He reaches behind his back to the counter behind him and retrieves a large bouquet of flowers. He hands them to me. My body stiffens and I resist the urge to squeeze my eyes shut as I remember the last one he gave to me.

"Again?" I say. "Didn't you hurt me enough last time you gave me flowers?" I feel my mouth tremble slightly as I speak. This moment means so much to me and I'm terrified that Slade is going to ruin it with one of his cruel barbed comments or another hateful gift.

"A lot has changed since then, Angel," he says softly. He looks down, but then steels himself and raises his gaze to mine. "I'm really sorry for how I treated you. That wasn't kind. You didn't deserve it, and it was more about myself than you. I want you to have these, to make amends for how I acted back then."

I take a deep breath, hoping this isn't a trick. Hoping it's nothing like last time.

Taking a closer look, the flowers are beautiful, including some I've never seen before. There are little yellow ones that I feel like I've seen growing on the side of the road, like wildflowers.

"Those are from the rue plant," he says, seeing me looking at them. "They symbolize regret and remorse. Seemed appropriate."

"They look too happy to represent something so dark," I say.

"Darkness can be deceiving. Darkness can be beautiful, too," says Brick.

"You're right. I've learned that from all of you," I reply, smiling at all four of them.

"So have I redeemed myself?" he asks, almost bracing himself at my potential response.

"Oh Slade, you'd already redeemed yourself," I say softly. "My guard was still a little up, just in case, because let's face it, you can be a bit unpredictable. Typical chef bullshit."

The others snicker, and then Slade himself smirks. "But this is very sweet, thank you. I appreciate the gesture, and I'll gladly erase the first bouquet from my mind and replace it with this one."

His shoulders noticeably relax. "Thank goodness for that," he says. "I promise I'll make it up to you for the rest of my life."

Chapter Thirty-One

Angel

"Now that you're free from Brett Wolf, but also from us, it's our life's work to make you never want to leave us. We will protect you at all costs, but not in a way that stifles you or pushes you away. We will adore you and treat you like a queen, because you are our queen. We will house you and feed you and spoil you, not because you're not capable of doing those things for yourself—because you are—but because we choose to do those things for you. We love you, Angel. We want you in our life, always. We need you. All of us need you. But it needs to be your choice to stay."

"Do you solemnly swear that each one of you will bury yourself deep inside my pussy and other holes upon request?" They all nod enthusiastically. Excellent.

"Will you grant me earth-shaking orgasms that rip through me and make my full body shudder and my toes curl?" They each nod some more.

"Will you tease me until I beg you to make me fall apart? Will you mark me as yours with bruises and welts and tattoos and piercings, in the perfect blend of pleasure and pain?" They nod again, and Brick gives me a double thumbs-up which makes me laugh. He liked that one a lot.

"And will you dominate me in the bedroom but always respect me, and remain faithful only to me? Even you, Roman? Are you capable of that?"

"Sure am," he smiles at me, and I can tell it's not his smooth player smile but that he genuinely means it.

"Sex aside, will you continue to embrace my darkness and encourage me to own the parts of myself that are emerging? To push my comfort zone and support me to be less beholden to false morals that people place upon themselves out of fear?"

"We one hundred percent will," says Aidan, the others nodding in agreement.

"Then I will happily remain committed to the four of you. As long as you uphold these vows, I am yours." I pause. "There are still many things about each other that we don't know. It hasn't been that long when you think about it. So I can't promise you forever. I know you want me to, but I can't. That would be foolish for me, for all of us."

I see their brows furrowing, concern palpable in their eyes.

"But I can promise that I will do everything I can to help you advance this empire. Our empire. One day, mark my words, we will overthrow Tane Brown and take control of these islands. People will say the Brixton name and shake in fear of our power, and Tane will seem like a tiny minnow. We will be the sharks. We will own these islands."

Relief washes over all of their faces. And respect. They can see that I truly want to support them in their quest, and they know I'm the right person to help them succeed.

"We got you something else," says Slade, glancing at the other guys.

"What? Besides the nicest hair salon that I've ever seen in my life?" They really are crazy. And crazy for me. I'm finally starting to believe it.

"Yeah, it turns out we enjoy spoiling the shit outta you, beautiful," says Aidan. "We think you're ready for it. And we will do everything to protect it as well as you."

Brick reaches into a cardboard box beside them I hadn't noticed before, and pulls out the most gorgeous black kitten I've ever seen. It has big blue eyes that dart about, assessing the environment for threats, food and things to play with.

"This is Brix," he says. "You can change his name if you like, but he answers to it already," he grins.

I smile as he hands the little squirming ball of fur to me. It looks deep into my eyes, assessing me, and then purrs. A low, soft purr of contentment as it snuggles into my arms.

"Hello baby!" I squeal, scratching him under his tiny chin with my forefinger, which only makes his purrs grow louder. "I like Brix," I smile at Brick and the others. "It suits him."

"Just like we suit you," he smiles back.

Chapter Thirty-Two

Angel

"**B**rick, you are fearless. You fall down hard, and you fall down often, but only to get right back up. And you are quirky as hell and it's adorable." Brick lifts his shoulders back and pushes his chest out, puffing himself up so he's even bigger than usual. He beams.

"Aidan, you are resourceful and responsible. You lead us through the most fucked up situations with grit and calm, and you always follow through. You're also sexy as fuck," I say.

"Roman, you're a complete charmer. You make people feel like they're the only ones in your room. But under the surface, there's more to you. You are truly kind. You put people's needs above your own, you're supportive and you intervene when you see people being treated unfairly."

"And Slade. Slade, Slade, Slade." Everyone laughs, including me. "There's just so much to say about you, isn't there? About us?" He smirks and nods.

"You are a fucking fantastic cook. You're argumentative and bitingly sarcastic, but you're also extremely perceptive. You're highly attuned to the unsaid, the gently implied. You're more empathetic than most people probably realize. You just choose to be an asshole with the information you have at your resourceful fingertips." Everyone laughs again.

"All of you are protective of me. Some might say possessive." I glance at them and they smirk, a couple of them shrugging. No denying it.

"But truly, you set aside your own wants and needs to make sure I'm taken care of. You make me feel like your priority. You make sure I'm safe at all times, and that nobody can cause pain. Except for you in the bedroom, which is different." I wink, and they all grin. A couple of them start to look a little horny.

"And you're also all incredibly hot. I have never experienced any one man, let alone four, who has made me feel so beautiful, so confident, so sexy, simply by being myself. You make me less inhibited, more willing and adventurous about trying new things. You're sensitive to how I'm feeling, and you know just how to bring me pleasure."

"So you don't have any regrets?"

"None whatsoever. I wouldn't change a thing."

CHAPTER THIRTY-THREE

Angel

Devon and I are furious. The guys got together to figure out next steps to take down Tane, but things got out of hand after what started out as a minor miscommunication, and they've all been bickering again. It's almost come to blows, and we're ready to intervene. This is nonsense.

"Stop all this talk about which group is right or wrong!" Devon cries out, as exasperated as I am. "You have to understand, everyone is morally gray to some extent. Some people are more obviously aligned with good or bad, but everyone has an element somewhere in between. In other words, nobody is truly all positive or negative, depending on the perspective you view them from. That goes for all of you, too!"

Devon eyes my guys. "You lot are willing to do whatever it takes to achieve your goals, even if it means hurting others in the process. That's why my guys have such a problem with you, because you'll go further than their boundaries allow to get what you want. But, from what I've seen, you also have a strong sense of loyalty and protectiveness towards those you care about, which is generally seen as a positive trait. That's something all eight of you have in common."

I double down. "All of you have complex histories that contribute to your moral grayness. Everyone here, including Devon and I, have made mistakes in the past and been forced into difficult situations where we've had to make tough decisions. In many cases, decisions we may not be proud of. Some of us are able to let it go, and the rest of us might dwell on those decisions for the rest of our lives. The decisions were still made, and we still have to live with the consequences."

I hand the figurative baton back to Devon. "Everybody here is complex. Nobody here can be totally categorized as good or bad. We all have flaws and have made questionable decisions, but every one of us also has redeeming qualities and I would go so far as to say we have all showed acts of kindness and heroism. So shut the fuck up trying to say this group is right or this group is wrong, or Angel and I will leave your dumb asses to fight in the playground while we go off and find some real men."

Everybody is silent. All eight men look sheepish, their eyes focused on the ground in front of them. They know they've fucked up.

"Well, fuck," says Aidan, running a hand through his hair. "I think they might have a point. We can agree to disagree on our approach, but one thing we can all agree on is that Tane Brown needs to be shut down, and he's the closest to evil anyone can get.

"Makes us all look like angels," says Skyler. He suddenly glances at Angel. "You know what I mean, not like a—."

I wave my hand and laugh. "I get it, I get it."

Chapter Thirty-Four

Angel

All ten of us stand on the beach, our surfboards at the ready as we gaze out at the gently rolling waves. Eight men and two women, two separate tight-knit groups now bound as one by our desire to take down Tane Brown and take over control of the islands.

The Brixtons, which now includes me and the cat, I guess. We didn't bring the cat. Maybe one day, judging by how courageous that little kitten already is.

And then Devon and the snakes.

I can barely believe we're in a truce with the fucking snakes, and we're about to join forces. This is wild, and none of us saw it coming until it hit us right between the eyes that there is no other way. But as difficult as it is to believe, and as challenging of a journey as it's been to get here, in this moment, it feels right.

As we wade into the water, we can feel the power of the waves beneath us, lifting us up and carrying us forward. Devon and I take the lead, carving a graceful path through the water as the men follow closely behind until we find a calm spot where we can turn and face the shore.

Looking around at this group, now sitting on our boards out in the ocean, I see strength, I see intelligence, and I see power in numbers. We're ready to make a plan to overthrow Tane Brown. And when the timing is right, we will strike. Together.

As the sun sets, the sky turns into a beautiful display of oranges, pinks and purples, casting a warm glow over the island in front of us. The temperature remains warm and inviting, and the sound of waves crashing on the shore provides a peaceful, relaxing soundtrack while we contemplate what's next.

This is a new era. This is the calm before the storm. And right now, there's no end in sight.

Also by Heidi Stark

Blood and Sand (Dark Reverse Harem Romance)

- Sea of Snakes

- Sea of Sinners

- Sea of Rage

- Sea of Pain

Billionaire's Takeover Collection

- Irreversible Decision

- Compelling Proposal

- Love Merger

- The Billionaire's Takeover Collection (all 3 of the above!)

Novellas

- Love in a Seedy Motel Room

Sign up for my newsletter herefor the latest on new releases, promos, giveaways and events!

Join me on social media:

Facebook: @heidistarkauthor

Instagram: @heiditstarkauthor

TikTok: @heidistark_author

Twitter: @heidistarkauthr

Website https://heidistarkauthor.com

ABOUT HEIDI STARK

Heidi Stark is an indie author specializing in contemporary dark romance.

She is inspired by the locations she visits on her travels, and the people she meets along the way.

When she's not writing, you can usually find her reading, listening to podcasts, or dreaming about her next book.

Learn more about Heidi Stark at her website. Sign up for exclusive content and my newsletter here.

You can also find out more about Heidi and her upcoming books on social media:

Facebook Page
Facebook Group

Tiktok/Booktok

Instagram

Twitter

www.ingramcontent.com/pod-product-compliance
Lightning Source LLC
Chambersburg PA
CBHW070511200726
48293CB00007B/2489

9 781960 630100